CHOSEN:

COMMANDER IN CHIEF

Judith Galloway

CHOSEN:

COMMANDER IN CHIEF

A Fictional Memoir by

JUDITH M. GALLOWAY

Columbus, Ohio

This book is a work of fiction. The names, characters and events in this book are the products of the author's imagination or are used fictitiously. Any similarity to real persons living or dead is coincidental and not intended by the author.

Chosen: Commander in Chief

Published by Gatekeeper Press
2167 Stringtown Rd, Suite 109
Columbus, OH 43123-2989
www.GatekeeperPress.com

All Scripture references are from the *Holy Bible, New King James Version*. Nashville: Thomas Nelson, 1982.

Second Edition, 2018.

ISBN: 9781642371666
eISBN: 9780692458297

Printed in the United States of America

"I don't know what your destiny will be, but I do know that the only ones among you who will truly be happy are those who have sought and found how to serve."

Albert Schweitzer

Dedication

To all women who have served, are now serving, or will serve their country in any branch of the armed services of the United States of America.

Table of Contents

Preface

ALTHOUGH THIS IS A WORK of fiction, many of the events are drawn from the author's personal experiences while serving as an officer in the United States Air Force. Some of the characters are real, some are fictional, and some are a combination of both. Events based on historical facts other than the author's own experience are cited as such in the notes.

JUDITH M. GALLOWAY

Prologue

I'M RUNNING OUT OF AIR. My lungs are on fire. Just one more lap. The quarter-mile track is crowded with other runners, most of them nineteen-year-old male cadets. I hear them pounding around the track on all sides. They're wearing white USAFA T-shirts with navy trim and navy-blue shorts. I'm wearing bright yellow running shorts and a Budweiser T-shirt trying to look cool. I considered wearing my Wonder Woman shirt but decided it would only antagonize. The cadets and I are trying to run three miles in twenty-four minutes to qualify for the freefall parachuting program. After six months of training my best time was twenty-six minutes. Thanks to the cadet jumpmaster pacing me, I'm ahead of the eight-minute mile pace. He's a wiry little guy about three inches shorter than I am with heavy-looking, black-framed glasses secured with elastic behind his head. I'm impressed that he's wearing combat boots. I tried that once and my hip joints were sore for days.

As I come around the final turn I feel a tremendous sense of relief. I'm going to make it! Thudding along the straightaway I hear the officer who has been serving as my lap counter call out, "One more!"

What? No! This was supposed to be the final lap! How can I possibly run one more? I don't have one more left in me! Did my lap counter deliberately sabotage me? I break stride and stagger to a walk. Cadet Haig, who has been pacing me, grabs my arm as I almost fall. "Come on, ma'am!" he urges. He begins running backwards so that he's facing me. "Come on, ma'am!" he repeats.

I know I'm losing valuable seconds, but my legs have turned to overcooked spaghetti. My husband, Bob, who has been on the sidelines cheering me on, joins Cadet Haig. They drag me around the first turn. At the halfway point I recover the self-discipline I learned from years of competitive swimming. I'm back on pace. As I round the final turn with only a hundred yards to go, I know I have to sprint flat out. I steel myself the effort and run wildly toward the finish line.

Everything begins to blur. I almost lose consciousness. Cadets who have finished well ahead of me begin cheering me on. Bob is at the finish line to catch me before I fall down flat like the walls of Jericho. I'm hyperventilating. My legs are burning with oxygen debt. As I stumble on I acknowledge the cadets with a wave and a cocky "Piece of cake!"

The timer calls out my time: "twenty-four minutes and twenty-three seconds." My heart, which has been sledge hammering against my chest, seems to drop to my stomach like a falling elevator. Tears course down my cheeks, mixing with sweat.

Bob is at my side. "Don't you dare cry," he scolds in a harsh whisper. "That's just what they expect." I bend over with hands on shaky knees and try to stop hyperventilating. Tears continue to roll down my cheeks. Maybe no one will notice. I'm suddenly nauseous. *Oh, God, don't let me throw up.* Bob walks me away from the track, where cadets are still milling around, trying not to look. Maybe some of them had been hoping I'd fail, but my final sprint seems to have won their respect.

The next day the Commandant of Cadets waives the twenty-three seconds off my time. It's important to test the feasibility of training a woman in the freefall parachuting program. Little did he realize that the first woman officer on his staff would almost die trying.

CHAPTER 1
The Call

San Francisco, January 2008

"WHAT THIS COUNTRY NEEDS IS an American Golda Meir," the professor began. His lecture was on "The Idea of a Woman President." The packed lecture hall of St. Ignatius College crackled with anticipation. Among the listeners was a journalist from the *San Francisco Chronicle*. As a political reporter, Harmon Ryland had a professional interest in the subject. He also had a personal interest as his sister-in-law, a retired Air Force brigadier general now serving in the U.S. Senate, could very well fill the role as the first American woman president. He just had to convince her to run.

Harmon was a student of history. He had been a young Washington reporter in 1969 when Prime Minister Golda Meir made a state visit to President Richard Nixon to request fighter airplanes to defend against Arab terrorism. What Harm admired most about her was her determination to promote the cause of Zionism against all odds.

Golda wore the sheen of a triumphant Israel and radiated moral certainty at a time when to be certain of one's morals was still honorable. Her often repeated mantra was, "Only those who dare, who have the courage to dream, can really accomplish something."1

Harm thought Rachel had the same kind of moral courage exemplified by the Israeli prime minister. He saw that she had the potential to serve her country in a role far beyond her own dreams or aspirations. His goal was to encourage her to see herself as he saw her. He decided to put the proposal to Rachel directly.

"Senator Ryland's office," the well-modulated woman's voice announced. After identifying himself, he was promptly connected to his sister-in-law.

"Harm, how are you? It's always great to hear your voice."

"Rachel, I'll get right to the point. What would you think about running for president?"

"You're not serious!"

"You're one of the best qualified people I know. Thirty years in the military, experience in foreign policy, and now four years in the Senate; you have what it takes, Rachel. We need a candidate who will capture the country's imagination. People are sick of self-serving politicians. We need someone who will fight terrorism with the same daring and courage that Golda Meir exhibited in the '60s and '70s. Please, just think about it."

* * *

Thirty years ago it was unusual for a young woman to join the military and unheard of to aspire to become president of the United States. Although she never dreamed of becoming the first woman president, Rachel did aspire to a military career.

Her father, a retired Air Force colonel, who had served during World War II and the Korean conflict, played an important role in her decision. The military values of honor, commitment, discipline, and self-sacrifice were a family creed. She admired the camaraderie she witnessed among her father's peers. Her overriding desire was to be part of an important mission.

During the late '60s when the majority of college students were demonstrating against the war in Vietnam, Rachel was writing articles for the Wellesley student newspaper in support of the war.

When her two male cousins fled to Canada to avoid the draft, she was galvanized into action. Two months after graduating from Wellesley College, she started Air Force Officer Training School (OTS) in San Antonio, Texas. The male-dominant environment was quite a change from the all-girls' schools she had attended. It didn't occur to Rachel to be intimidated by this. She assumed once she was commissioned she'd be accepted as part of the group. For her it was all about the mission.

Following OTS, Rachel completed Avionics Technical Training at Lowery AFB, Colorado and was assigned to the 12th Flying Training Wing, Randolph AFB, Texas. There she met her future husband, Captain Bob Ryland, a combat veteran and T-38 instructor pilot. He graduated from the Academy in 1966 and did two tours in Vietnam flying F-105s. His blond hair and blue eyes made a nice contrast to Rachel's dark hair and hazel eyes. Both were tall and athletically built. They were a couple worthy of a recruiting poster. Bob had classic Scandinavian good looks. His high forehead reflected his intelligence. His square jaw bespoke determination to overcome any obstacles. He spoke with quiet authority in a deep baritone which immediately commanded attention. Rachel's dark hair, heavy lashes and brows were courtesy of her Scottish ancestry. Her strong chin and high cheekbones set off her delicate nose and mouth. Her smile radiated confidence.

As one of the few women officers at Randolph, Rachel quickly came to the notice of the wing commander, Colonel Hoyt S. Vandenberg. The colonel was over six feet tall with aristocratic features only slightly marred by severe acne scars from his younger years. He had wavy brown hair with only a few threads of grey. He was a West Point graduate and a fighter pilot's fighter pilot. Rachel admired him to such a degree that she would become tongue tied in his presence. He became her mentor. In 1973 he was promoted to brigadier general and reassigned to the Air Force Academy as commandant of cadets. The following year, when pressured to add a woman to his staff to plan for the admission of women cadets, General Vandenberg called Rachel in San Antonio.

"Rachel baby," the general began, "how soon can you get up here?" Her heart skipped a beat.

"Is two weeks soon enough, General?"

"I'll have your orders cut immediately. Give my regards to your husband." Rachel slowly hung up the phone.

"Oh, my God! What will Bob think?" With shaking hands she called his squadron. As usual, he was flying. Her astonishing news would have to wait.

That night Rachel was too excited to eat the special dinner she'd made to celebrate.

"It's a great opportunity for you, honey," Bob said with obvious pride. "Here's to the first woman officer on the staff of the commandant," Bob toasted, raising his glass of Chardonnay. "You'll make history."

Rachel's cheeks were flushed from the wine. "I don't know whether to be excited or scared to death. I'm just a junior captain. Aren't most of the staff senior captains and majors?"

"That's true but don't worry. Once you get oriented, you'll wax their tails!"

"Spoken like a true fighter pilot. It's a good thing I got my thesis written last month. A master's degree in Aerospace Systems Management might help me to compete."

"General Vandenberg wouldn't have chosen you if he didn't think you could do the job."

"We'll be separated for six months plus the time you'll be in training with United. It's going to be hard to leave the familiarity of the maintenance squadron and be separated from you at the same time."

"It'll give us longer to sell the house," Bob rationalized. "If we get a buyer right away I can live in the BOQ until I go to Houston to train on the DC-8.

"I guess we'll work it out. I'm so glad I married you. The prospect of facing four thousand male cadets would be daunting if I didn't have you backing me. Being a grad, you know how cadets operate. With your insight I won't be as naive as they expect."

CHAPTER 2
The Academy

NEWS OF RACHEL'S ASSIGNMENT PUT her on the front page of the base newspaper. She had little time or inclination to enjoy her sudden celebrity, however. Two weeks later she was adjusting to her new assignment at the Air Force Academy as the first woman offier on the staff of the Commandant of Cadets. Only two other women officers were assigned to the Academy. Both were former intelligence officers. Lieutenant Colonel Holmes taught French and Major Jensen taught History.

For the first month Rachel called Bob almost every night to discuss the details of the day. It reduced her insecurity. He helped her navigate the tricky waters of being the only woman in a sea of macho males. Rachel felt like the wave of the future continually crashing against a wall of male hostility.

It was February and the air was cold and dry. It had taken Rachel several weeks to adjust to the 7,000 foot altitude at the Academy. It was quite a change from San Antonio which was closer to sea level. In spite of her focus on the plan for the admission of women she took time to touch base with her family. Her parents were intensely proud of her selection as the first woman on the staff of the commandant. At the end of her first month Rachel called her sister, Susan, to wish her happy birthday and share her news. They only spoke about twice a year.

Susan lived in Boston with her husband who was a Physics professor at MIT. While they were growing up Susan had as little as possible to do with her little sister. She seemed to find her a nuisance when she wasn't busy criticizing her. Sometimes walking home from elementary school together Susan would sock her in the arm for no apparent reason. Whenever Rachel would ask for help with a homework problem she was treated like a moron. She was always trying to measure up. When teachers at their Catholic girls' school realized she was Susan's little sister they would always ask, "Are you are smart as your sister?" Rachel would always reply, "No, I'm the cute one. She's the smart one."

Rachel was not surprised when Susan was too busy to talk to her on the phone. After telling of her new assignment, instead of congratulating her, her sister passed it off as not particularly interesting.

"Thanks for letting us know where you're stationed," Susan said. "But I suppose you'll be separated from Bob for a while, right?" It seemed Susan was always looking for the negative in any situation. Even though it was probably unconscious the implied criticism cut Rachel to the core. "Yes, but we hope to get together every few months."

"Did you know that I just got a promotion at work?" Susan asked with more enthusiasm.

"Yes, I just talked to Mother and Dad and they told me. They were very happy for you." Rachel was then treated to half an hour narrative about her sister's position as a senior computer programmer at Arthur D. Little which was a ground breaking computer software company in Cambridge. That was finished off with another lengthy narrative about her husband, Tony. He was head scientist on a new contract with NASA. When Rachel finally hung up the phone she felt belittled and unimportant.

After three months of intense concentration on the plan for the admission of women, Rachel welcomed the arrival of spring break. She and Bob were looking forward to skiing in Aspen. He flew up to Colorado Springs from Randolph on a T-38 cross-country with one of his students. It was late afternoon when the "white rocket" made a picture perfect landing at Peterson Field just south of the Academy. The snow on the 14,000-foot summit of Pikes Peak stood out in silhouette against the setting sun. The air was dry and cold. Rachel waited patiently on the tarmac outside Base Operations in her dress blues and high heeled black kid pumps.She shook slightly from the chill breeze, or was it nervous anticipation?

After dismissing his student, who would stay at Peterson Field during the layover, Bob spotted his wife. A wide grin lit up his handsome face as he swept to her side.

"I sure have missed you, honey," Bob said as he squeezed her hello by his side with his flight bag in the opposite hand.

"Missed you more," Rachel replied after a quick but heartfelt kiss. They were always careful about public display of affection in uniform.

"Are you ready for some skiing?" Bob asked as he got behind the wheel of Rachel's new Bronco.

"More than ready. I need a break from the zoo. I just hope we don't run into too many cadets in Aspen."

"Who cares? It'll give them a chance to see you're a happily married lady." Rachel felt her face get hot.

"I already have a reputation as a workaholic, but that's a requirement for everyone who works for the commandant."

"How is the general?" Bob inquired. He'd known Vandenberg at Randolph and, like Rachel, always admired him.

"He's the same as ever. You know his motto: 'Live fast, die young, and make a good-looking corpse.'"

"That's every fighter pilot's motto," Bob chuckled as he pulled up to their duplex in Douglas Valley, where most of the married commandant's staff was housed. Until their household goods could be shipped, their quarters were furnished with only the barest necessities borrowed from the base housing office. After leading him up the stairs from the carport, Rachel spread out her arms to the empty livingoom.

"Here it i," she said her voice echoing off the walls. "What do you think?"

"Hmm. Spartan. Do you have a bed?"

"Of course, follow me." She led him to the larger of two bedrooms. They shed their uniforms with the practice of seasoned professionals. By midnight they had made love twice and got up to had bacon and eggs. A few hours later they were on the road to Aspen.

As the sun rose, the snow-clad mountains blushed like a bride. "I feel like we're on our honeymoon," Rachel said. "The one we never had time to take."

"And we're going to make the most of it!" Bob replied.

Rachel and Bob first met at a Junior Officer's Council meeting at Randolph AFB, Texas in 1973. She was a first lieutenant and he was a captain. They fell in love almost immediately and determined that they would find a way to make their marriage work in spite of Air Force policy which didn't preclude separation. They understood this. For both of them the mission would always come first. It was hard wired into their DNA. They were both sold out to the mission. Rachel never had any doubt of her calling as a military professional. She'd always been very independent and believed she could make it in a male dominant environment despite the sexual harassment and discrimination.

Robert Ryland was an Academy grad and never expected to resign his commission after his initial commitment. Every grad is required to serve on active duty for eight years to repay the government for its investment. This was only just. Robert thought he would be a fighter pilot until his eyes failed and then he would be content to push paper. He secretly hoped to become Chief of Staff of the Air Force one day. After his disillusionment with the way the war in Vietnam was conducted by the politicians in Washington, he simply could no longer support a career in the military. His distrust was too deep. However, he never inflicted his disillusionment on his wife.

Following an afternoon of skiing they settled in front of the fire in their cabin.

"Three more months and I'll be finished with my eight-year commitment and off to fly the friendly skies."

"Any regrets?" Rachel asked as she looked into the blue eyes she loved.

"None at all. After Vietnam my ideals have been pretty well shattered. I'll still fly in the Reserves, but I'll leave active duty to you." Rachel knew it wasn't the reality of war that had shattered his ideals, but the hypocrisy of politicians who continued to fight a war they didn't know how to win.

"You know I plan to make the Air Force a career," Rachel said, looking for support.

"It'll be a lot easier with only one of us on active duty. We won't have to worry about joint spouse assignments when you're transferred," Bob said. "Wherever you're stationed I'll always be able to fly home. I think we can handle it."

"I know we can," she said with more confidence than she was feeling.

CHAPTER 3
Stress Training

WHEN BOB RETURNED TO SAN Antonio, Rachel plunged back into the plan for the admission of women. She decided to research other previously all-male training programs that had recently integrated women.

In 1974 the Los Angeles Police Academy began training women for the first time. With the commandant's approval she and another officer made a visit to see what problems they were having. Although the women were meeting the same standards as the men, it didn't change male attitudes. While they might respect their ability in training, no one wanted a woman for a partner. Did the men worry that the women would cave under pressure, or was there another reason? Would the close relationship be a sexual threat? Rachel had naively believed that if a woman completed the same tough training she would be accepted as a co-professional, but mere competence wasn't enough. The women would have to prove they wouldn't undermine good order and discipline.

A study published in 1973 described the performance of thirteen women pilots who underwent NASA's Initial Mercury Astronaut Testing Program. She was eager to share the results with Bob during one of their frequent phone calls.

"Listen to this," Rachel began. Quoting from the study she read:

"The tests included measurement of the effects of vertigo, performance under high G-forces, profound sensory isolation, and simulated crash landing. In the opinion of the scientists evaluating the results, women were deemed as capable as men for space flight, in some ways more so. They were more radiation resistant, and more durable in the face of loneliness, heat, cold, pain, and noise."1

"That's good to know," Bob responded mildly.

"Aren't you impressed?"

"Yes, but I'm not really surprised. After all, I've seen what you can do."

"The sad part is that even after the women performed so incredibly none of them were selected to be astronauts. Back in 1959 I guess the culture wasn't ready for coed crews in the space program," Rachel said.

"Things are changing gradually," Bob said.

"You can't prove it by me. Everyone is so negative here. The admission of women cadets is about as welcome as an invasion of aliens. It's not only the cadets but the staff as well. Even the wives are against women but for different reasons. The men think women will degrade standards. The wives don't want their husbands spending more time with cute little women cadets than they do with them."

"Hang in there and keep up the research. It sounds like you can make a good case for the performance of women cadets. They might even raise standards instead of lowering them."

"That's what I think too," Rachel replied.

"How're you getting along with your boss?"

"Colonel Hill has been very supportive, but I don't know what his true feelings are toward women. I try not to come on too strong with him."

"That's wise. You don't want him to think you're a flaming feminist," Bob kidded, knowing this was a hot button issue.

"You know I'm not! Besides it's not up to me to argue for the integration of women. It's just up to me to make it a success."

"Hey, you know I'm on your side, babe. I'll be on terminal leave in another few months and we'll be together for three weeks before I go to multi-engine training with United."

"I can't wait. Thanks for being such a good sounding board. If I couldn't blow off steam, I'd erupt like a geyser."

"Take care of yourself. I'll call you next weekend. Love you."

"You too." She hung up the phone feeling encouraged but as lonely as ever.

One month later Rachel began having severe pain in her lower abdomen. Her primary care doctor referred her to a gynecologist at the base hospital who performed a biopsy. The result indicated endometriosis. The doctor explained the condition is caused by a spontaneous shedding of the uterus which results in endometrial cells clogging the Fallopian tubes and sometimes enveloping the ovaries. This is what causes pain.

"What's the treatment?" Rachel asked.

"Well, you can go on the birth control pill without interruption for about a year to simulate pregnancy. That will stop the spontaneous shedding of the uterus. Or you could get pregnant, which accomplishes the same thing," he stated placidly. He had been assigned to the Academy hospital for eight years and primarily treated the wives of active duty service members. He wasn't used to treating active duty females. He was unaware of the unique challenges of a career professional like Rachel.

Going on the birth control pill for a year sounded very unnatural to her, and it went against her Catholic conscience. She simply replied, "That won't work for me. Becoming pregnant while I'm blazing the trail for women cadets would definitely send the wrong signal even if it were feasible with my husband being stationed hundreds of miles away"

"If the ovaries are involved it may not help anyway. The only other alternative is to have a complete abdominal hysterectomy."

In spite of the impact of so drastic a choice Rachel's immediate reaction was to focus on her mission. "How long will it take me to recover?"

"Six weeks is usually enough time to resume your normal activities."

Would that include running the bayonet assault course? "I need to talk to my husband about this."

"If you decide to go ahead with surgery I can work you in next week," he said matter-of-factly.

Although they'd discussed having children someday, Bob agreed this was not the opportune time. Since their career paths caused them to be geographically separated there really wasn't any other choice even though it was upsetting. In the end they decided it was best to take care of the situation before it developed into something more serious. After all, they reassured each other, they could always adopt. Most women would become depressed with the loss of their child-bearing capacity. Rachel didn't dwell on it. Getting on with the mission was her primary concern.

As Bob's terminal leave was still months away he couldn't be with her when she went through the surgery. She awoke in the recovery room blinking at the bright lights and shivering in the chill temperature. Her abdomen was seared with pain. Her throat was raw from the NG tube placed during surgery. She was allowed ice chips to suck on but nothing to drink. The first three days were the worst. After that the pain was bearable until she tried to get out of bed. Walking to the bathroom, she was bent over like somebody's grandmother.

"I've totally lost all military bearing," she told Bob on the phone. She was glad he couldn't see her like this.

"I'll bet the cadets would love to see you gimping around the corridors," Bob teased.

"Nothing like a little moral support to comfort the wounded," Rachel replied.

When she was feeling stronger she called her parents in New York, who were unaware she was even ill. Tactfully, neither of them said anything about the loss of future grandchildren. They were only concerned for her well-being.

Five days after surgery she was sent home and told not to climb stairs or do any lifting for several weeks. A neighbor came by to help during her convalescence. General Vandenberg even called to wish her a speedy recovery. She assured him she was working on a design for the women's uniforms while at home.

By the time she was able to return to work it was July. The second phase of basic cadet training had begun in an area north of the academy called Jack's Valley. One of the big questions about training women concerned their ability to run the obstacle course, the confidence course, and the bayonet assault course. The officer staff wore green fatigues and royal blue ascots for this phase of training. The Air Force didn't make fatigues for women, so Rachel bought a pair of men's fatigues and had them tailored to fit her narrow waist. She was a distracting sight when she appeared at the training area in her bloused boots, fitted fatigues, ball cap, and pilot's sunglasses. Unaware of the stares from the cadets, she thought she'd fit right in.

After observing training for a few days, she decided to attempt some of the obstacles herself. A major from her department, who was particularly macho, was monitoring the "Slide for Life" on the confidence course. Her sore abdomen made it painful to climb the thirty-foot tower. As she looked down the cable she would ride to a point ten feet off the ground before dropping off, it no longer looked like fun. It just looked scary. She cast a glance backward at the major standing below as a first-class cadet hooked her harness to the cable. She clenched her teeth and jumped.

"Good job," the major commented as she completed the slide. "I could tell you were pretty scared. You turned white up there, but you did it anyway. I respect that."

It was a watershed moment. She realized the way to gain acceptance from the men was to complete as much of their military training as possible. She knew she couldn't do it all, but she had an idea. What if a small cadre of young women officers went through the training? It would gain credibility for women cadets, and later the women could serve as a surrogate upper classmen. She waited for the right moment to present her idea to the commandant.

CHAPTER 4
Camaraderie

WHEN SHE WASN'T OBSERVING SUMMER training, Captain Ryland was tasked with revising the curriculum for the Command Communications course which she would be teaching in the fall. Another instructor worked with her on the project. Captain John Mauss was a C-130 pilot. He was built like a basketball player; too tall to be a fighter pilot. Like all rated officers on the staff, he had flown in Vietnam. His Midwestern accent matched his easygoing personality. He wasn't handsome but had an endearing grin when something amused him. He had a high forehead and a large nose. His sandy blond hair was always just a little too long and usually ruffled. He had a habit of running his fingers through it when he was thinking hard. He carried himself with loose-jointed assurance. John stood out among his peers because he didn't appear to have any animosity toward the admission of women. While working with John, she found the camaraderie she had sought. After the duty day one Friday in the fall John stopped Rachel in the hall outside their offices.

"How did your classes go today, Rachel?"

"The cadets really liked watching the video of the Patton speech," Rachel replied. "Of course, they already realize the importance of a military commander being able to inspire his troops on the eve of battle. I was pleased they could dissect the elements of the speech that made it work. People who have seen the movie with George C. Scott don't realize that the speech he gave was really a distillation of two speeches that General Patton gave prior to the final push into Germany."

"Using the video clip was a real motivator. Too bad we don't have the film of MacArthur's farewell speech to Congress," John said.

"Maybe we can get a copy for next year," Rachel replied. "The audio tape is so dramatic, though, I think the cadets will be mesmerized just by the sound of MacArthur's voice."

"You're probably right about that," John agreed.

"The cadets are all so bright and motivated. It's really a pleasure to teach them."

"If you think they're motivated in class, wait till you see them at the game tomorrow."

"I'm looking forward to it. Bob's driving in tonight and he's coming with me," Rachel said with a shy smile.

"I know you're looking forward to being together. Being separated from your spouse is hard for any of us," John said. During my two tours in Vietnam, Jan waited anxiously at home with our two toddlers."

"It's only been six months but it seems like longer. It'll be good to have him home."

"Since we both live in Douglas Valley, why don't we drive to the game together?"

"That would be nice. I look forward to seeing Jan again. She was such a big help to me while I was convalescing."

"See you tomorrow then. We'll pick you up at thirteen hundred."

Bob arrived at their quarters late Friday night. Rachel was ready to greet him wearing a new silk nightgown. It had the desired effect. The fatigue of the fourteen-hour drive melted away at the sight of her. When they came up for air it was 1 a.m. As usual they had scrambled eggs and went back to bed.

The next day the packed stadium was electric with anticipation. The cadets in their dress blue uniforms and service caps formed an impressive block of support for the home team.

John and Rachel were also wearing dress blues as required by all staff members. It was a pristine fall day, perfect for the first game of the season. The aquamarine sky set off the Rampart Range and Pikes Peak in high resolution. As the cadet marching band took to the field during halftime, the two pilots traded stories about their Vietnam experiences. The two women also took the opportunity to chat. Jan was about the same age as Rachel. She had the solid build of a field hockey player which two pregnancies had done little to alter. She had a pleasant face and wore her light brown hair in a youthful pony tail. She carried herself with confidence. Rachel asked Jan about her two children.

"John Jr. is such a little man," Jan said proudly. "Even at seven he's so protective of Jimmy. I'm glad they're close enough in age to do things together."

"Did you plan it that way?" Rachel asked.

"God planned it that way, I guess," Jan said.

"Do you think you'll miss not being able to have children, Rachel?"

"I guess we will someday, but right now we're both so caught up in our careers we haven't had time to think about it," Rachel answered, a little too quickly. Jan hoped she hadn't been tactless.

"How are the guys treating you at the office?" Jan asked to change the subject.

"John has been a real friend, but most of them resent me being there, and they don't make it any secret. I try not to take it personally. In a way I don't blame them. I went to an all-girls high school and college and I wouldn't want boys admitted there either."

"But the Academy is different, isn't it?"

"Yes, it is," Rachel said, surprised at Jan's insight.

"It's about equal opportunity for advancement," Jan continued.

"That's right. Women officers deserve to have the same professional education as men provided they can meet the same entry requirements. The thing that women like Senator Pat

Schroeder don't grasp is that it's not about equal rights. It's about equal responsibility. Both men and women have the responsibility to serve their country to the very best of their ability, and that includes receiving the best military education they can."

"I bet you're sick of the argument that the Academy trains combat leaders, and women can't serve in combat, therefore they have no place at the service academies," Jan said.

"It might be a good argument except that forty percent of the grads don't serve in combat specialties. I'm against women in combat for the simple reason that by their very presence women could compromise good order and discipline. There is nothing I'd like better than to fly an F-16 in combat, but once you put women in coed aircrews you run the risk of rivalry among the men for the woman's attention. Then there is the additional issue of the jealousy of the wives. The intimacy of crew closeness would put an additional strain on marriages, which in turn would undermine readiness. Women like Pat Schroeder who've never been in the military don't know what they are talking about when they want to pass the equal rights amendment. Fortunately the legislation to admit women to the academies is separate from the equal rights amendment."

"What's the current status?"

"It looks like we'll be admitting women in 1976."

"It's a good thing the commandant brought you on board early. You'll have time to plan for a successful transition."

"You know, Jan, you're the only wife I know who has a positive attitude toward the admission of women. No wonder John and I get along so well."

"I think the other wives are just insecure and maybe a little jealous."

"Present company accepted, I hope," Rachel replied, hoping she had guessed right.

"John and I met at OTS."

"You never told me, Jan." Rachel realized she'd been too self-absorbed to even ask about Jan's background.

"We got married as soon as he finished pilot training and were lucky to get a joint spouse assignment when he went to upgrade training in B-52s. That's when I got pregnant with John Jr., and you know the rest of that story."

"Yes, I do," Rachel replied. "As you know, they changed that policy last year. Do you think you would have stayed in, Jan if you'd had the choice?"

"I think I would have at least for a while. But I can see now that I never could have combined raising children with an Air Force career."

"What were you doing before you got out?"

"I was the WAF squadron commander at Barksdale. I really enjoyed that position, but it breaks your heart to hear how so many of the enlisted women are sexually harassed."

"I know what you mean. When I was at Randolph one of my friends had the WAF squadron, and she told me stories that made me want to castrate the men who preyed on naïve young airmen. I'm doing my best to make sure that doesn't happen to the women cadets."

"I'm all for it, but how do you think you can do that?"

"Well, for one thing, I've been reading about the integration of women at other previously all-male colleges. According to two female sociologists, who wrote a book about women at Yale, a sort of incest taboo develops when women are in the same dormitory. The men become protective instead of predatory.[1]

"That's interesting. Let's hope it works the same way here."

"Amen to that," Rachel said.

"Oh, here come the teams again," Jan said. "Looks like halftime's over."

CHAPTER 5
The Plan

THE MAIN BUILDINGS IN THE cadet area are set around a large marble square known as "the Terrazzo". The buildings were designed in a distinctive, modernist style, making extensive use of aluminum on building exteriors, suggesting the outer skin of aircraft or spacecraft. Captain Rachel Ryland strode across the terrazzo from her office on the commandant's side to the academic building where she taught her military studies classes. Her highly polished black kid pumps tapped rhythmically on the white marble. Her dress blue uniform was newly adorned with the Air Force Commendation medal conferred by her former commanding officer at Randolph and pinned on by the commandant in an early-morning staff meeting.

Cadets swarmed toward her while headed to different parts of the cadet area. Each one rendered a sharp salute, which she returned with equal snap. One of the things Rachel enjoyed most about the Academy was the strict military bearing of the cadets.

When she entered the classroom, the cadet nearest the door called the class to attention, rendered a salute, and stated, "Ma'am, the class is prepared for instruction." In the beginning the cadets kept saying "Sir," which always made her smile. They were more embarrassed at their mistake than she was.

In spite of her success in the classroom, Rachel knew she wasn't accepted as a co-professional by her peers or the cadets.

In one of her frequent night time phone conversations with Bob she talked about her feelings.

"How can I compete with a staff of pilots and navigators, all of whom have served in combat?"

"Rachel, I understand your concern," her husband responded.

"One of my fellow instructors is even a Medal of Honor winner!"

"There's no way for any nonrated officer to compete with pilots and navigators, especially those who have flown in combat. What do you think the solution is?"

"Even though I've been doing some flying at the aero club, I know that isn't going to hack it. I have to somehow show I have the kind of guts cadets can relate to."

"Uh-oh. What are you thinking, my gutsy girl?"

"I think the next best thing to flying airplanes is jumping out of them. Freefall parachuting is the one program I can go through that all cadets respect. But there are two problems."

"What are they?" Bob asked.

"It's going to be tough to pass the physical qualifying test. I'll have to run three miles in twenty-four minutes and do eight pull-ups."

"I remember. As you know I went through the training as a third-class cadet. But you can do anything you put her mind to. What's the second problem?"

"My boss is an experienced jumper himself. I've already approached him with the idea and he thinks it's too dangerous."

"Well, there *are* risks," Bob agreed. "What if you're injured? Or worse, what if you bounce?"

"I thought you were on my side?"

"I am, but I can see his point of view."

"I think I can convince him that it's important to test the feasibility of training women cadets."

"Okay, babe. Go for it!"

Rachel finally persuaded her boss to allow her to at least train for the qualifying test. The commandant was delighted with the idea, as she knew he would be. He even asked the Athletic Department to assign a coach to help her train.

Captain Dave Martin was an Academy grad. He'd known Bob Ryland as an undergraduate although they were a year apart. Dave had the emaciated build of a serious runner. Rachel met him at his office in the field house to discuss a training program for her. She was pleasantly surprised to find he'd already been working on the development of physical standards for the women cadets. He was an expert on physiological differences between men and women. As a result he had come up with the concept of "equal level of effort."

He explained, "Due to lower center of gravity, fewer red blood cells, and less muscle mass, a woman's performance of eight chin-ups is the equivalent of eight pull-ups for a man."

"Do you think cadets will buy that?" Rachel asked.

"They'll have to because it is going to be policy," Dave replied. After you get changed I'll meet you at the indoor track and we'll see what we've got to work with."

Rachel had been a competitive swimmer in college, but she'd never been a runner. She kept in shape by doing laps in the indoor pool at the cadet gym. At least she thought she was in shape until Captain Martin started to lead her around the track at the eight-minute mile pace.

Breathing heavily after the first few laps, Rachel said, "This is going to be a little tougher than I thought."

The indoor track was popular during the lunch hour when the officer staff normally did their workouts. A giant timer with a sweep second hand was mounted on a pole on the side of the track in front of the bleachers. Apparently she wasn't the only one interested in precisely timing their laps.

After half a mile Dave slowed down to a walk to allow Rachel to catch her breath. "Interval training will help you to increase your speed," he explained. "The idea is to run the straights and walk the curves. Let's try it." For the next thirty minutes Dave coached her while she practiced running intervals. They finished up with some stretching exercises.

"Okay, ready for the weight room?" Dave asked.

"I've never done any weight training," Rachel said, somehow feeling apologetic but not knowing why.

They made their way from the track in the field house through an underground tunnel to the weight room in the gym. Wearing sweatpants and T-shirt, Rachel instantly saw she was in the wrong uniform. Bare-chested men proudly displayed their well-developed pectorals as they sweated through their workouts. It created an intimacy that jarred her.

Captain Martin led her to the chinning bar. It reminded her of the bars on the playground in elementary school on which she used to perform one-legged spins with her skirt blowing around her. She could still visualize herself in a flying dismount. The image in her mind was a stark contrast to the reality before her.

As expected, she could just barely perform one chin-up. With great patience Dave demonstrated a series of weight training exercises to increase her upper body strength. He coached her as she performed each exercise. Keeping in mind her long-range goal, she swallowed her self-consciousness and tackled the weights with as much determination as she did every other aspect of her job.

Bob Ryland started flying as first officer on DC-8s at the same time Rachel began training for the jump program. She missed him when he was flying three weeks out of every month, but was so exhausted at the end of each day it was a relief not to have to prepare dinner. She existed on protein drinks and sandwiches with an occasional meal at the commandant's table in the cadet dining hall. On days when she did her running in the early morning she sometimes joined her fellow officers on the "staff tower," which overlooked four thousand cadets in the dining room below.

One day at lunch the commandant asked Rachel if she'd like to learn the manual of arms. He didn't know that thanks to Bob's coaching she'd already been practicing with the M-1 Garand. To avoid painful bruising by the nine-and-a-half-pound rifle, she'd put pot holders under her bra straps.

"So, what do you think about training cadets in a little close order drill?" Vandenberg asked.

"Whatever you think, General," Rachel answered, not sure if he was serious.

The general seemed to enjoy the prospect of seeing cadets on the drill pad performing for a woman. Then he began quizzing Rachel on different drill and ceremonies terms.

"What's the difference between distance and interval?" he asked as if grilling a cadet. Rachel's mind was suddenly blank. She felt her face go hot with embarrassment. The male officers at the table smirked to one another, enjoying her humiliation. She'd always loved drill and ceremonies at OTS and prided herself on her performance as she led her squadron on the drill pad. Where was her mind?

"Maybe we'll hold off for a while on having you drill cadets," General Vandenberg remarked laughing along with the other men.

Rachel vowed she would never again fail a test of military knowledge. She got a copy of the little red book that cadets were required to memorize and studied it. She never had occasion to display her knowledge, however. The general didn't quiz her again and he never again brought up the subject of drilling cadets Rachel thought it probably just as well.

During their regular one-on-one sessions a few weeks after the lunch on the staff tower, Rachel brought up the idea she had conceived in Jack's Valley. "General, I think what we need is a pilot study to prove to the cadets that women won't lower standards."

"I agree," the general said, pleased with the idea.

"We could recruit young women commissioned through OTS and ROTC and put them through a compressed program of all the physical and military training cadets are required to complete. Afterward they could be used as a surrogate upper class. They would not only help to train women cadets, they would serve as role models."

"The Air Force Academy used recent grads from West Point and Annapolis as surrogate upper classmen to train the first male cadets in the 1950s," the general said. "I think they were called Air Training Officers." Vandenberg was not one to hesitate to make a decision. "From now on your job will be to recruit and train women officers to serve as ATOs. I'm going to reassign you directly to the vice commandant. You'll need to be ready to implement the program in January as women cadets will be admitted in July of next year. I'm relieving you from your instructor duties, but I want you to continue to develop staff studies on the issues related to the women cadets. I'll assign two other officers to assist you."

"Yes, sir! Thank you, sir."

Rachel left the office with a renewed sense of optimism. She'd already worked with Colonel James P. McCarthy, the vice commandant. They were continually rewriting the briefing on the plan for the admission of women.

The colonel was a highly decorated fighter pilot who'd flown 152 combat missions in Vietnam. He was short and wiry, the perfect build to fit in an F-4 cockpit. In spite of his macho image, however, he had a positive attitude toward the integration of women. Rachel had met his attractive wife, Alice, who was a registered nurse and the mother of their six children. She was on good terms with Alice McCarthy which was fortunate as Rachel would be e spending a lot of time with her husband.

Rachel could hardly wait to tell Bob about the new plan.

"What we are hoping to do," she explained, "is to compress four years of physical and military training into six months. We'll recruit fifteen women second lieutenants and ask them to project into the role of cadets. We plan to use first classmen to train them. They'll live in one of the dorms in a segregated hallway. After basic cadet training they'll continue with fourth class training followed by each successive year of military training."

"Aren't you worried that the men will be too hard on the ATOs, hoping to see them fail?" Bob asked.

"Actually, the research I've done shows that when men train women for the first time they tend to be too easy rather than too hard. Of course there are exceptions. The group commanders will handpick the members of the cadet cadre. We'll only use first classmen with proven leadership ability, plus they'll have to be volunteers of course. My staff and I will be supervising the training to watch for any problems."

"What about fraternization?"

"Good question. Of course it will be forbidden, just as it is between upper-and lower-class cadets. It might be more difficult to enforce, but I think we can make it work."

"What are you looking for in the women you're recruiting?"

"We'll give preference to women in nontraditional career fields since they will serve as role models, and it will be important for them to project both strength and femininity. We'll start by asking Military Personnel Center to create a list of lieutenants with not more than two years on active duty. We want them to be in their early twenties and single, of course. Then we'll refine that list for those in nontraditional career fields.

"I'll be conducting telephone interviews to establish initial interest. Those who want to be candidates for the program will come to the Academy for an interview. While they're here they'll have to pass the same physical fitness test we give basic cadets. If they pass they'll be given a battery of psychological tests. The finalists will be interviewed by one of the group commanders and the vice commandant."

"Sounds like quite a time-consuming process," Bob remarked.

"It will be. But the idea of putting the ATOs through a training program that simulates the physical and military training that cadets go through is so that the cadets will see them succeed without lowering standards. When that happens we expect the negative attitude of the wing to change.

"It just might work," Bob said.

"Enough about me. How do you like flying the DC-8?"

"It's not nearly as exciting as flying a fighter, but the pay and benefits are a lot better. I'll begin flying the Houston-Washington-Chicago route next month."

"How's your roommate?" Rachel asked knowing that her husband was sharing a furnished apartment with another former Air Force pilot.

"Jack's a good guy. He flew KC-135s so the transition's been a lot easier for him.

"What do you guys do on the weekends?"

"Study flight manuals mostly."

"Right. All day and all night."

"Well, we go out for happy hour on Friday nights and sometimes we play a round of golf on Saturdays," Bob admitted.

"Didn't you tell me Jack's recently divorced?"

"Yeah. His divorce was final just before he got out of the Air Force. He's still pretty broken up about it."

"People sometimes have a rebound romance right after a divorce," Rachel observed. "Did that occur with Jack?"

"Not yet, but I think he's working on it."

"So the two of you are hanging out in Houston singles bars, huh?" Rachel asked.

"Well, like I said, we go to happy hour on Friday nights. If he meets someone he's interested in, I come home alone and what he does is his own business."

"Just make sure you don't meet any sweet young things that are prowling the bars for unattached airline pilots," Rachel admonished.

"You're not jealous, are you?"

"You bet your sweet ass I am."

"Don't worry, honey. None of them can hold a candle to my captain."

"That's *so* reassuring," Rachel said.

CHAPTER 6
First Jump

C APTAIN RACHEL RYLAND SAT ON the floor of the jump plane. The U-4B , an Air Force version of the Aero Commander L-26 was used by President Dwight D. Eisenhower from 1958 to 1960 for short hops. It was the first presidential airplane to have only two engines. When President Eisenhower left office the U-4B was transferred to the Air Force Academy to be used as a jump plane.

Four cadet jumpers were bunched up like grapes, knees to chest. Captain Ryland and Major Ted Sullivan, the OIC of the jump program were the only officers on board. The cadets were nineteen-year-old third classmen. Rachel had just turned thirty.

Aside from cadet rank, the parachutist badge was one of the few tangible signs that distinguished a cadet from his peers. For the rest of their careers the coveted jump wings would mark them as Academy grads.

The pilot leveled out over Colorado Springs and headed northwest at 150 knots toward the Rampart Range west of the Academy. The August sky was as blue as lapis lazuli punctuated by white fluffy cotton ball clouds.The pilot would maintain an altitude of ten thousand feet. The Academy is over six thousand feet above sea level at the airfield so the actual height above ground at which the jumpers would exit the aircraft was four thousand feet.

Rachel tried to keep her eyes averted from the gaping hole in the fuselage where the door had been removed. As the plane circled over the cadet area, she glanced down at the cadet wing marching across the terrazzo to the dining hall in the noon meal formation. The white spires of the cadet chapel gleamed in the August sunshine like seventeen fixed bayonets pointed up at her in defiance. She knew most of the cadets were hoping she'd bounce on her first jump. Through successful completion of the program, she hoped to gain their respect and maybe even their acceptance as a co-professional.

As the last squadron disappeared into the dining hall, the plane banked into a final turn and headed east toward the drop zone. Gazing at the open doorway, Rachel felt a surge of adrenaline kick up her heart rate. Above the noise of the aircraft the cadets yelled brave jokes to each other as young men do when they're frightened but don't want to show it. She wanted to join in the camaraderie but didn't trust her voice to be steady.

One by one the cadets exited the aircraft. The pilot circled the drop zone one last time. It was finally her turn in the door.

"*Coming on range*," the jump master commanded as the red light on the bulkhead came on. Rachel shifted her body with crab-like movements toward the open fuselage. The bulky MC-1 backpack and reserve belly chute made her movements awkward and jerky. The air was cool at ten thousand feet, but Rachel felt sweat pouring down the back of her flight suit.

"*Get ready*," commanded the jump master. Her legs became those of a rag doll dangling in the 120-knot prop wash. Her heart gyrated like an out-of-control Ferris wheel. She took a couple of slow, deep breaths, planted her right hand on the floor, and grasped the side of the doorway with her left. The final command came, "*GO!*"

The captain hurled herself out of the airplane turned ninety degrees and hit a perfect hard arch. She might have been diving off a platform ten feet above the water instead of four thousand feet above the airfield.

On the ground a group of cadet jumpers gathered around the NCOIC of the program, Chief Master Sergeant Holder. He was watching the jump through tripod-mounted binoculars. The chief was a merciless critic. During ground training he had fed her magazine articles on female parachuting fatalities, trying to scare her out of the program. He also made it almost impossible for her to be checked off on parachute landing falls.

The average cadet is checked off in four hours. Unlike the male cadets who were used to the rough and tumble of football, Rachel hesitated to collapse and roll when she hit the pea gravel. After nineteen hours of parachute landing falls (PLFs), the chief refused to check her off. Finally, Major Ted Sullivan, the OIC of the program, took over. They worked together in the Military Training Department. He passed her.

The final phase of ground training is the thirty-four-foot tower. Bob Ryland happened to be home during the last week of his wife's training. To provide moral support he accompanied her to the training area. Tower jumps are designed to simulate the sequence of events in an actual jump.

Two safety lanyards are attached to the parachute harness. One holds the body close to the tower. The other is attached to an overhead cable. After leaving the platform and turning ninety degrees in a hard arch, the body is dropped two feet from the cable. The jumper then performs the count-and-pull procedure. This is followed by the release of the first safety lanyard and a ten-foot drop to simulate opening shock. After the jumper reacts to various emergency situations, the second lanyard is released, which allows the jumper to slide down the cable, dropping off in a PLF on a mound of sand.

Rachel's first tower jump was satisfactory. Buoyed with confidence she climbed the tower for her second jump. This time an equipment malfunction caused her to fall twelve feet instead of two feet after exiting the tower. In spite of the intense shock to her spine, she held her hard arch thinking it was just a test of her ability to react to an emergency situation.

"It's okay, Captain," one of the cadet jump masters advised. The second safety lanyard was released and she slid down the steel cable, dropping off into a PLF.

On the third tower jump the equipment malfunctioned again. Instead of being suspended close to the tower after the initial two-foot drop, Rachel went zinging down the cable and ricocheted off a cross wire strung between two telephone poles. She hung suspended like a string puppet flung about by an angry child. Naively, she assumed this was just one more test of her ability to react to an emergency.

By this time Bob Ryland was convinced these malfunctions were a deliberate attempt at sabotage. He silently ground his teeth in rage.

"You can relax, Captain, we'll get you down," one of the cadets yelled. Some minutes later a ton-and-a-half truck was driven underneath her. One of the cadets climbed on top of the cab and flipped open the capewell covers to release her harness. When she reached the ground, Major Sullivan commented wryly, "Well, we'd better put you out of the airplane before we kill you on the tower."

Rachel rode in silence to the drop zone, which was about ten minutes from the ground training area. The cadet trainers strapped her into the MC-1 backpack and reserve belly chute. Before she had a chance to think about it, she was boarding the U4-B with four cadet jumpers and Major Sullivan acting as jump master. They were quickly airborne.

Her exit from the aircraft was flawless. Her diving training enabled her to hold her hard arch while experiencing the exhilaration of freefall for the first time. Looking up into the empty blue of the August sky gave her no point of reference. It felt like slow motion. There was no sense of the 125 mph terminal velocity, just the incredible feeling of flying her body. The flapping sound of the wind blowing her flight suit against her legs was barely audible through her helmet. She went through the count-

and-pull procedures as she'd rehearsed countless times on the freefall body position trainer.

"One thousand...two thousand...three thousand...four thousand...look thousand...reach thousand...pull thousand." Rachel pulled with her left hand while balancing her body position with her right arm extended. Nothing happened. She immediately thought *hard-pull procedure*. Reaching across her chest with her right hand she pulled the blast handle with both hands. The pins that held the canopy tightly in place were immediately released.

She was unaware that she had pulled on her back. The few seconds during which she executed her hard-pull procedure had destabilized her body position. She rolled over, causing the chute to open underneath her and wrap around her in a "horseshoe" malfunction. If not immediately corrected, it could be fatal.

Two minutes later she landed in scrub oak, dangerously close to the taxiway. Rachel felt a sharp pain in her left forearm. Was her arm broken? No, only a sticker piercing her flight suit. Major Sullivan, who had jump mastered her, landed a few feet away, having been the last to exit the aircraft. He ran over and enveloped her in a big hug.

"You did it!" He seemed almost as relieved as she was that she hadn't bounced. Rachel was too stunned to reply. They field packed their chutes and trudged over to the parachute loft, where Rachel would receive a critique from her nemesis, Chief Holder.

As soon as she reached the loft she saw Bob beaming at her from a respectful distance. She wanted to run to him and collapse in his arms, but she maintained her military bearing to face her critique.

"You pulled on your back, you know," the chief said pulling his fire plug body up to its full 5 foot 6 inch height. He had a derisive grin on his face. "The parachute wrapped around you like a shroud. The only thing that saved you was wind shear."

"Oh," Rachel responded weakly, turning pale. She removed her helmet and ran her hand through her short brown hair which was plastered to her scalp.

"You'll have to complete five more hours on the freefall body position trainer to correct that problem."

"I see."

"Also, you reached for the ground. That's a good way to break your legs. That'll be five more hours in the PLF pit."

Oh, goody. Feeling drained, Rachel merely nodded. After she stowed her chute in the loft Bob drove them back to their quarters. That night he carefully didn't mention his belief that she had been deliberately sabotaged on the tower. He figured she had enough to think about after having almost bought the farm on her first jump. He did, however, have an explanation for her deliverance from what could have been a fatal, fast-moving malfunction.

The unpredictable crosswinds at the Academy prevented the Indians from settling there. Ironically, what they believed to be evil spirits had actually been providential. A crosswind had blown the chute off when it had wrapped around her like a shroud.

The near death experience shook her but also gave her courage. After all she'd been through in the training she had no doubt that God was in control. As she fell asleep she was no longer afraid but humbled and grateful. God brought her safely to this point; she trusted he wouldn't abandon her now.

After remedial training on the freefall body position trainer and five more hours in the PLF pit, Rachel was ready for her second jump. The one part of the first jump that was perfect was her exit and hard arch, but for some reason she developed the idea that it was just luck and not skill. Consequently, she lacked confidence during her second exit from the airplane. She performed a backward loop which delayed her count and pull procedure.

As an extra precaution, an automatic firing device had been attached to her main chute in addition to the customary one on the reserve.

What was designed for her safety created injury. The two-second delay of her backward loop caused the automatic firing device to explode just as she went in for the hard pull. It was as if her jaw received a vicious left hook with brass knuckles, throwing her head backward and sideways.

Nothing was said about this irregularity except the firing device was eliminated from her main chute on subsequent jumps.

Rachel carefully didn't admit to any injury, but Bob took her to a physician off base to assess the damage. X-rays revealed two compressed cervical discs. The doctor warned her to stop jumping or risk becoming a quadriplegic. She thanked him but mumbled to herself, "You don't understand the situation." She'd rather break her neck than not complete the program.

CHAPTER 7
Air Training Officers

ONE WEEK AND THREE JUMPS later the Academy superintendent, Lieutenant General James Allen, wearing dress blues, trudged through the scrub oak holding a pair of silver jump wings. A grinning Captain Rachel Ryland stood at attention while a news photographer captured the moment.

"You've just become the first woman in the military to complete the Basic Freefall Parachuting Program," the lieutenant general stated with a broad smile as he pinned the jump wings to the front of her flight suit. "Congratulations." Overwhelmed with joy and relief, Rachel was speechless for a moment.

She replied weakly, "Thank you, General."

From then on the superintendent seemed to take great pride in presenting Captain Ryland to every distinguished visitor who came to hear her briefing on the plans for the admission of women. After preliminary remarks about the common training program, he'd always smile at Rachel and say, "We even have them jumping out of airplanes."

Captain Ryland resumed work on the design of the ATO Training Program as well as identifying issues related to integration. By the time the first women were admitted, she and her staff had studied over one hundred problems and recommended solutions to the commandant. It was grinding work. Although frequently plagued with severe headaches from her cervical injury, Rachel took work home with her every night.

As a result of this work and the ATO program, the Air Force would have the lowest attrition rate of the three service academies

In January 1976 the ATO Training Program began with a press conference held in the large briefing room in Doolittle Hall. Captain Rachel Ryland was the keynote speaker. She sat with composure next to the Academy superintendent and the commandant of cadets. She was a polished speaker and this was a subject on which she had spoken often. On either side of the lectern the fifteen ATOs were arrayed in their dress blues. It was a pretty picture. They sat demurely while press photographers clicked their cameras.

The ATOs were an impressive group by any standard. They had been selected from over two hundred women lieutenants identified by the Military Personnel Center. The first second lieutenant Captain Ryland had contacted by phone was Second Lieutenant Rhoda Sweitzer, who was stationed at Altus AFB, Oklahoma, as a maintenance officer. She was immediately interested and became the first prospective ATO to come to the Academy for an interview. Rhoda was a champion water skier and looked the part. Her blond hair and blue eyes reflected her German ancestry. She was athletically built and radiated a quiet competence. Captain Ryland knew immediately that she had found her first ATO.

The most senior ATO was Charlotte Green, another maintenance officer. She had just been promoted to first lieutenant. She was chosen by the vice commandant to be the first ATO commander, a leadership role that was rotated three times during the six-month training program.

At the opposite extreme was the youngest and most junior ATO, Yardley Nelson. She had graduated from Mississippi State, where she had been commissioned through ROTC. Yardley was the only black ATO. She had been a star runner in college and was attending Air Traffic Controller School when she was selected.

The only ATO from a traditional career field was Paula Gathright, who was immediately dubbed "the poor man's Elke Sommer." She was a willowy blond administrative officer. During a swimming workout at the beginning of training, she struck her head on the side of the pool while doing the backstroke and failing to execute a turn. The resulting neck injury plagued her with severe headaches for the duration of the training program, but she never complained.

Another ATO who experienced a back injury during the program exhibited the same courage. She ignored her pain and completed the training. It was vital that none of the women be eliminated from the program. The whole idea was to change perceptions of the cadet wing. All of the women had to show the qualities of discipline and perseverance that were expected of male cadets. The tendency for women to over achieve in an all male environment was well documented by the research Captain Ryland had performed. She worried about the injured ATOs. She understood well what it was like to ignore physical pain for the sake of the mission.

The basic cadet portion of the ATO curriculum was in some respects the most challenging because it was when the women experienced the most culture shock. They were stripped of their rank and forced to project into the role of basic cadet. Their hair was cut very short and they were clothed in green fatigues and combat boots. They were addressed as "Miss" or "Cadet" instead of "Lieutenant."

The cadet training cadre had been selected with as much care as the ATOs. It was their job to ensure the ATOs were subjected to the same emotional and physical stress as male cadets. If an ATO failed to recite "knowledge" correctly from the cadet handbook she would be braced against a wall and reprimanded. If the error was particularly egregious she would be instructed to drop and perform ten push-ups.

Captain Ryland often observed the cadet cadre as they did uniform inspections prior to marching the ATOs to breakfast.

One morning ATO Dawn Reed was put in a brace as a first classman yelled into her face, "Is that what you call a spit shine, Cadet Reed?"

"Sir, no sir!" she replied. The diminutive ATO stood against the wall at a stiff position of attention. Deceptively fragile-looking at five feet, four inches, she held her own against the tirade.

"Are you going to put out for me, Cadet Reed?" he shouted.

"Sir, no sir! We are not allowed to fraternize with upperclassmen," she answered with a perfectly straight face. The upperclassmen smothered a gagging sound to keep from breaking up. It was all over the wing before the end of the day. The incident provided welcome comic relief for the ATOs and the cadets.

The second phase of ATO training included parasailing and soaring. It was a nice break after the regimentation of basic cadet training. The women performed well and were highly motivated to tackle the classroom airmanship and navigation courses that were part of the third-class curriculum.

One of the major milestones in cadet training is Survival, Escape, Resistance, and Evasion (SERE, pronounced *Sear-ee*). This training is conducted in the bivouac area north of the academy and usually takes place in the summer. It involves living off the land and spending nights under makeshift shelters. Snow was on the ground when the ATOs went through SERE. In spite of the harsh environment, they performed well.

The POW compound phase is recognized as the most emotionally stressful and psychologically challenging of all cadet military training. By this time the ATOs were highly proficient at role projection and seemed to have no trouble identifying as POWs. Captain Ryland was concerned they might break under the pressure. She needn't have worried; none of them did.

By the end of May all fifteen women lieutenants had completed the program. Their success gained substantial credibility for the future women cadets.

CHAPTER 8
Sheppard AFB

ONCE THE FIRST CLASS OF women cadets successfully completed basic cadet training, Captain Ryland was selected to attend Squadron Officer School at Maxwell AFB, Alabama. Before beginning the three-month school, Rachel and Bob managed a short vacation in the Bahamas. They flew down on a United flight out of Denver. Warm, moist air redolent of hibiscus and bougainvillea greeted them as they exited the airplane. It was a welcome change from the cold, thin air of Colorado.

In spite of the immediate joy of being with Bob, Rachel experienced an emotional letdown after three stressful years. It wasn't as much a relief as a sense of loss. After all the furious planning and eager anticipation of the first women cadets, she wondered if she would ever again experience such a sense of achievement. At the same time, she had become so obsessed with her role at the Academy that she felt guilty that she had put her relationship with Bob on the back burner. Even though he never complained and fully agreed that the mission came first, she wondered how she could make it up to him.

While sunbathing on the beach one afternoon Rachel hesitantly brought up the subject of adopting a child. "I realize we need to make a decision while we're still young enough to be good parents."

"With my flight schedule and the demands of your career, I don't see how it's feasible to raise a child. Not unless one of us changes careers," Bob offered.

"Are you suggesting that I get out of the Air Force?" Rachel asked. Even though she had considered it, she was automatically defensive.

"No, of course not, but I guess it's either that or I have to stop flying."

"I can't imagine either one of us giving up the careers we love."

"Why don't we wait a while longer before we decide? After all we're both still in our thirties," Bob said.

"I guess you're right," Rachel agreed.

Just then a dark cloud passed in front of the sun, signaling the rapid approach of a tropical storm. The beach cleared out in minutes. The absence of light left them both with an inexplicable sense of loss.

After her Academy tour, Rachel had been singled out for special career monitoring and rapid advancement. She completed Squadron Officer School but not in her customary position at the top of her class. She was not only recovering from physical exhaustion, but she couldn't seem to shake a growing feeling of ambivalence.

Her next assignment was to Sheppard AFB in Wichita Falls, Texas, as commander of an aircraft maintenance student squadron. As an avionics officer she looked forward to the maintenance training environment. The Texas location put her much closer to Bob, who was based in Houston.

Bob had been flying copilot on a four-engine DC-8 for three years when the aircraft lost an engine on approach to Chicago O'Hare International Airport. As a former combat pilot he was no stranger to in-flight emergencies. Later, he related the incident to Rachel.

It was pitch black outside. The crew had sweated out two hours of flying on three engines. After notifying the air controllers of the emergency, they were cleared for an immediate approach. On final about fifteen miles out with no hydraulics in the number one system, the pilot began to let down.

Ryland screamed, "Engine fire!" Red warning lights and fire bells poured confusion into the cockpit. The pilot pulled back the power on the burning engine and discharged the Halon. This made it necessary to keep extra pressure on the left rudder to make up for the yawing of the airplane to the right. He lifted the flaps, which had been in the down position for landing, to firewall the power on the remaining engines.

When the fire was out they landed safely.[1]

"Nice job, Captain," Bob remarked. He'd been flying with Captain Nick Sarkesian for only a short time. He'd found him to be thoroughly professional but unusually taciturn for a former Air Force pilot.

"You didn't do so bad, yourself," Sarkesian replied.

That was the beginning of a lasting friendship. Sarkesian had been flying the DC-8 since 1973. He and his wife, Linda, lived in Houston, where United was based. Nick was a Texas A&M graduate. He met his wife there and they married upon graduation. He was average height with a swarthy complexion and a brooding personality. Linda was a rosy-cheeked blond whose outlook on life matched her coloring. Nick invited the Rylands to join his family for Thanksgiving. Rachel welcomed the invitation. It would be nice to be part of a family celebration.

After dinner while the guys were watching football, the women talked in the kitchen as they cleaned up after the meal.

"How long have you two been married?" Linda asked.

"We got married in 1974 when Bob was still on active duty. We were both stationed at Randolph in San Antonio. That makes it five years."

"Do you ever think about getting out of the Air Force?" Linda asked.

"I'll be hot for oversees when I finish this tour at Sheppard." Rachel replied, avoiding the question. "We're hoping I can get Hickam or Yokota and that Bob can successfully bid the Hawaii-Japan-Philippines route," she said, trying to sound nonchalant.

Linda's houseful of kids was a pleasant domestic scene, but Rachel couldn't put herself in the picture. She wondered if her husband envied Nick. Outside the kitchen window she watched the men playing catch with the boys. Rachel knew Bob would make a great father. She wondered if he ever considered divorcing her and marrying someone who could give him children. Did he love her enough to stay in the marriage without children?

She thought about offering to give him a divorce. Did she love him enough to give him up? They had both been raised Catholic and married in the Church. Neither of them believed in divorce. Yet, she wondered.

Unlike most of his airline peers, Bob was never unfaithful in spite of frequent opportunities. They had avoided the subject of adopting a child since their trip to the Bahamas. The problem didn't have a satisfactory solution as long as he was flying and her career looked so full of promise.

Rachel returned to Sheppard eager to put aside personal concerns and concentrate on the task of managing a five hundred-person student squadron. She loved the training environment. These men and women were straight out of basic training. They'd been in the Air Force six short weeks, not quite enough time to assimilate the values of the military. Part of her challenge as a student squadron commander was to inculcate those values.

Since the draft was abolished at the end of the Vietnam War, the all-volunteer force had a distinctly different makeup. There weren't as many recruits from big cities, where job opportunities were more numerous. Many came from family farms, where they had already absorbed the values of hard work and discipline. The Air Force offered them a chance for technical training and adventure. This made it easier to motivate them.

As women's role expectations changed during the early '70s, more of them considered service in the military. When the draft was ended the quotas for women almost doubled to make up for the shortfall in male recruits. This allowed women to form a critical mass within the training squadron rather than being segregated in an all-female squadron as they had been previously.

When Captain Ryland assumed command of the 3763rd Student Squadron it had the worst disciplinary record of any in the training group.

The previous commanding officer had been a transport pilot who tried to run things like a flying squadron. As a result, discipline was lax and the number of trainees being discharged soared. Rachel intended to change that.

Fortunately, she had a competent staff of NCOs to help her. Her training superintendent, Technical Sergeant Bill Hurley, a former Marine, didn't believe in coddling. He had a face like a bulldog and a personality to match. Now that he was unhindered by a commander with loose standards of discipline, he came down hard. Sometimes, Rachel thought, he was almost too hard. She suspected when Hurley decided a trainee wasn't Air Force material he would hound him until his record of disciplinary infractions justified discharge. By the time the trainee got to the squadron commander there was not much she could do to rehabilitate him.

There were 475 men in the squadron and twenty-five women. In a formerly all-male career field like aircraft maintenance, it pleased Rachel that the women often outperformed the men. It was a common scenario. Women had to perform twice as well to be accepted as equals. A student leader from each class was chosen by the training superintendent based on performance. When Captain Ryland assumed command the student leader was a petite blonde from St. Louis. Airman Lucas was a strict disciplinarian and an excellent leader.

Not all of the men liked Airman Lucas, but they all respected her –all except one. Toward the end of the three-month training course Airman Lucas found a dead cat hanging outside her dormitory window. Hysterical, she reported the incident to Technical Sergeant Hurley, the training superintendent, who had one of the junior NCOs dispose of the body.

It didn't take long for the culprit to identify himself. Airman Ripley, who was already awaiting discharge for dealing marijuana, proudly confessed to the crime. Ripley was a mousey-looking little guy with glasses. He gave the impression that he lived mostly in his own head, where undoubtedly various criminal plots were always dancing about like stars. He was a haughty intellectual and considered himself smarter than most people. None of his peers liked him. As tough as Hurley was on discipline, he wanted no part of Airman Ripley. He promptly reported the situation to Captain Ryland and left it to her to take action.

It was obvious the airman was potentially dangerous and possibly mentally ill. He belonged in the psychiatric ward of the base hospital. She could have called the security police to escort him, but she didn't want to handle it that way. Instead, she personally drove him to the base hospital. On the short drive Captain Ryland tried to make small talk. Airman Ripley seemed to be unconcerned about their destination. She kept thinking he would do something violent or bizarre, but he just sat in the vehicle chatting pleasantly. Even though the car's air conditioning was on, she felt like she was suffocating in the humid air.

At the hospital Ripley didn't even show any resistance when she walked him to the lockdown unit. It was almost as if this had been his plan all along. It suddenly occurred to her that maybe she had played right into his hands. Even so, she clearly had no choice but to place him into custody. She rang the bell for admission to the psychiatric unit. Hurley had called ahead so the medical staff knew they were coming. After Ripley was admitted without fuss, Rachel collapsed on a nearby chair in the corridor. Her legs were suddenly too shaky to support her.

CHAPTER 9
Police Blotter

THE FIRST THING CAPTAIN RYLAND read each morning was the police blotter from the previous day. As a new class of airmen arrived each week, a class graduated. With the help of her NCOs the squadron was beginning to turn around.

One Monday morning while reading the blotter she discovered that five of her airmen had been arrested for starting a riot. Several airmen were taken to the hospital and the instigators were in the confinement facility.

"Oh, God!" the captain groaned aloud. She called her training superintendent to brief her on the details. He was at her office in less than a minute.

"Well, ma'am, as you see it happened Sunday night at the Airmen's Club," Hurley began. "Apparently one of our female airmen was being harassed on the dance floor by a male from the 65th Squadron. One of our guys grabbed him and threw him against the bar. Several of his buddies came to his defense, which promptly led to a fistfight. What could be more natural, right?"

"Go on."

"Then some of our guys got a hold of pool sticks and started whaling on 65th guys. That's when the security police arrived."

"There is something you're not telling me, isn't there?"

"Well, ma'am, there was an additional factor," Hurley admitted with his bulldog grin.

"The other guys were black, weren't they?"

"That's right, ma'am."

"No wonder they escalated out of control. I want the record of every airman who was arrested as soon as you can assemble them."

"Got 'em right here, ma'am," Hurley said as he handed over the folders. "The unfortunate thing is all of them were about to graduate."

"What's your recommendation?" Captain Ryland asked, although she already knew what she wanted to do.

"Well, ma'am, as you'll see from their records, none of these airmen have been in any trouble before. And their academic records are above average. They'll be held in correctional custody awaiting court-martial. They were so close to graduation, the government has a lot invested in them. They probably shouldn't be discharged, just busted to basic airman and fined. That and the time in confinement is probably sufficient punishment."

"With the way legal is backed up, it'll take weeks before they come to trial. They'll have to be washed back in training. I wish we could just discharge them without waiting for the court-martial," the captain remarked.

"Yes, ma'am, but you know how the system works."

"Unfortunately, I do. Thank you, Sergeant Hurley." As he left the office she picked up the phone to make an appointment with her boss, the group commander. He also read the blotter every morning, and she would have to brief him as soon as possible.

CHAPTER 10

Crash of Flight 173

U NITED FLIGHT 173 TOOK OFF from Stapleton International Airport in Denver en route to Portland. Bob Ryland, flying copilot, was about to face the crisis of his life. The aircraft was on approach. It had been a routine flight, but when Captain Nick Sarkesian lowered the landing gear, a loud thump was heard.

"What the hell was that?" Bob exclaimed.

"Feel that vibration?" Sarkesian replied.

Even more alarming was the abnormal yaw of the aircraft. Both pilots saw that only two of the green landing gear indicator lights came on.

"I'm going around while we figure this out," Sarkesian said in a calm voice. Bob notified the control tower of their difficulty and was cleared to circle the area. The cockpit crew was so focused on the landing gear problem that no one noticed the fuel gauge. After several minutes they were no closer to solving the gear problem. Fuel continued to ebb away. Incredibly, the aircraft circled in the vicinity of Portland for nearly an hour.

Suddenly Bob shouted, "We're flying on empty!"

"Prepare for crash landing!" Sarkesian announced to the passengers and crew over the PA system. There were screams and cries as passengers and crew members braced for the crash.

The plane ran out of fuel in a sparsely populated area killing ten and seriously injuring twenty-four of the 189 on board.[1] Two flight attendants died. Bob Ryland and the flight engineer sustained serious injuries.

Nick Sarkesian miraculously escaped injury. He called Rachel at eight p.m. from the Portland Medical Center. He explained about the crash and told her than Bob was in surgery and in serious, but not critical, condition. She immediately arranged for-emergency leave and took the redeye flight from Dallas to Portland.

When she reached the hospital the next morning Bob was still in the recovery room. Rachel was allowed to visit him but only a few minutes. She was shocked at how white his face looked. The surgery caused him to lose a lot of blood. His eyes were closed. She wasn't sure he was awake.

"I'm here," Rachel said softly, squeezing his hand gently. His eyes opened slowly.

"Hi, babe," Bob croaked through a throat that was still raw from the NG tube that had just been removed.

"How do you feel, sweetheart?"

"I can't remember much about the crash," he managed to say, still fuzzy from the morphine.

"Don't think about it for now. Just rest. I'll be in the waiting room with Dave."

"Is Dave okay?"

"Yes. He was very lucky. Try to sleep now," she said softly, caressing the side of his face, as he drifted off into the blessed fog of the painkiller.

Sarkesian filled Rachel in on the details of the crash. A few hours later Bob was moved to a private room. She and Dave came in as soon as visitors were permitted.

"How many people were killed?" Bob asked. Nick told him. Both of them were still in shock. The loss of two crew members was particularly grim news. There wasn't much either of them could say. It was such a stupid accident.

Weeks later the National Transportation Safety Board investigation revealed what had happened. The right main landing gear retract cylinder assembly had failed due to corrosion and that allowed the right gear to freefall. Although it was down and locked, the rapid and abnormal freefall of the gear damaged a micro switch so severely that it failed to complete the circuit to the cockpit green light that tells the pilots that the gear is down and locked. It was those unusual indicators that led Sarkesian to abort the landing so they would have time to diagnose the problem. It was ironic that if it hadn't been for the malfunctioning light, none of those lives would have been lost.[2]

Nick Sarkesian and Bob Ryland were temporarily grounded pending the outcome of the accident investigation. When it was determined that the cause of the accident was due to pilot error Nick Sarkesian committed suicide. Suffering from severe depression himself and struggling to recover from back surgery, Bob decided to quit the airlines. His overly developed sense of responsibility led him into a morbid sense of guilt.

There was no question that the families of the deceased passengers would bring a lawsuit against the airlines. Other similar accidents had taken place before the United disaster, some of them involving even greater loss of life. As a result of the crash of Flight 173, United Airlines instituted the industry's first cockpit resource management program in 1980. This program proved so successful that it was adopted throughout the world.[3]

CHAPTER 11
Rachel's Dilemma

RACHEL WAS ABLE TO TAKE two weeks leave in order to take care of Bob during his first weeks of convalescence. They were both shocked by the news of Nick Sarkesian's suicide. There was nothing Rachel could say to comfort Bob. At first, coping with his physical pain helped divert his mind from the depression he felt over the loss of his friend and his own flying career.

Bob spent most days watching old movies on TV and walking their two dogs, Charlie and Rascal. The dogs were their surrogate children. Charlie was a golden retriever mix and Rascal was a border collie. Charlie had been unwanted and abused by a neighbor who was only too glad to let Bob have him. Rachel found Rascal one morning on the side of the road on the way to the base. She took the puppy to the squadron, where she was immediately adopted by the trainees as a mascot and attended all squadron softball games.

Rachel was glad that the two dogs were at home with Bob to provide company and comfort. Although her duties at the squadron kept her from focusing solely on Bob, she grew more and more desperate to help him. He had started drinking heavily and occasionally became verbally abusive. His face appeared drawn and deep grooves had appeared around his mouth and between his eyes. He had lost ten pounds.

Even before the accident Bob had stopped going to church as his flight schedule made it almost impossible. Now if she so much as mentioned going to Mass on Sunday he erupted in a verbal tirade.

Two months after surgery he seemed to sink into a black hole. Rachel felt helpless. Her former sense of satisfaction from her work wasted away. She had begun to grind her teeth at night. Her jaw was so sore she sometimes couldn't eat without pain. Her weight had dropped some, but she tried to be vigilant about her own health in order to stay strong for Bob. As was her usual resource when feeling depressed, she started attending daily Mass at the base chapel. A small group of civilians and military personnel made up the congregation on weekdays. The group became close-knit. It provided some shelter from the storm of her emotions.

Rachel realized she had made the mistake of thinking she was in control of her life. After her near-fatal parachute jump at the Air Force Academy she thought she had surrendered her life completely to God. When had she taken it back?

Why did it always take a crisis to wake up to the reality that God alone was in control?

Seeking guidance, Rachel asked the Catholic chaplain for an appointment. Father Wozniak was the son of Polish immigrants. He was tall and lean and possessed a wonderful sense of humor that endeared him to his congregation. After serving as an intelligence officer in Vietnam, he got out of the Air Force to attend seminary and then joined the chaplain corps. His Vietnam experience made him especially sensitive to the problems of combat veterans.

"Father, every day I pray to be able to surrender my life more completely, but I feel like I'm in a spiritual desert, in the midst of a sandstorm. I don't know where I'm going anymore." Rachel told the chaplain about her sense of helplessness in the face of her husband's depression. She outlined Bob's military experience and the crash of United Flight 173.

"Bob has recovered physically from his injuries but not emotionally. I can't reach him anymore. At first I thought his anger and depression were just temporary reactions to the accident. He wasn't fired by the airline; he chose to give up flying because he felt so guilty about the loss of life."

"Very understandable."

"Then he started having nightmares, some of which involve flying in combat."

"My guess would be that the airline crash triggered flashbacks to his combat experience. It sounds to me like he has post-traumatic stress disorder," Father Wozniak stated. "But I'm not a psychologist. The VA clinic has someone who is an expert in PTSD. Veterans get individual counseling and are encouraged to attend a weekly support group. It seems to help most of them."

"Bob is very private. I don't think he'd participate in a support group let alone get individual counseling."

"All you can do is let him know what is available. The rest is up to him."

"Maybe God is using this to show me that I need to give up my career and become a full-time wife," Rachel said. " I could always get a job teaching."

"How many years do you have in?"

"Just over nine."

"You're almost at the halfway point. That's a big investment. How would Bob feel about you doing that?"

"He would be against it."

"It also would put another load of guilt on his shoulders, wouldn't it?" the chaplain replied.

Rachel looked into his kind Polish face. "I didn't think of it that way."

That evening after dinner Rachel told Bob what Father Wozniak had recommended.

"*What*? You talked to the chaplain about me? What gave you the right to do that?" His eyes widened, then narrowed with simmering rage.

"I went to him because I feel so helpless. I don't know what to do anymore. I can't seem to reach you. It scares me." Rachel felt her whole body stiffen. Tears filled her eyes.

"There is nothing you can do! I don't want to discuss my feelings with you. And I definitely don't want to talk about them to the chaplain or some self-pitying support group!"

"I love you. I can't bear to see you like this!" Rachel exclaimed as tears ran down her face.

"The subject is closed." Bob got up from the dinner table so suddenly he almost knocked the chair over. His face was distorted with grief and anger. He grabbed the dog leashes off the hook by the front door.

"I'm taking the dogs for a walk," he said, slamming the door as he left.

Rachel sat still for several minutes. His reaction was not unexpected. She wondered if she had made matters worse. All she could do was pray.

"I can't help him, Lord. Only you can bring him out of this pit. Help me to be patient and to keep my hands off the problem. I am turning him over to you. Please keep us in your will."

Her assignment at Sheppard was coming to an end. She was expecting an overseas tour. The timing couldn't be worse. Bob would need to establish himself in a new career, and so far he didn't seem able to decide what to do. He toyed with the idea of going to law school, but his self-confidence was so undermined that he never got around to filling out an application.

Rachel again considered leaving active duty. She could join the Reserves and avoid any further separations. At the same time if he continued his abusive behavior she would welcome a remote tour. She felt guilty that her own career was going so well, but she knew one of them had to work. Her anger led to resentment. Maybe she had unrealistic expectations, but she certainly didn't want Bob to become a camp follower. The role of house husband didn't suit him at all. It didn't suit her either.

CHAPTER 12

Tornado

ONE TUESDAY AFTERNOON IN APRIL Captain Ryland was conducting parade practice with her squadron on the apron of the aircraft hangar where maintenance training took place. The sky began to darken and rain looked likely. Deep-surface low pressure was winding up over southeastern Colorado, bringing gusty winds and very moist air northward into what would become a storm zone. A dry line, a boundary between extremely dry air and ground moist air, was developing to the west of Wichita Falls, providing a focal point to spawn thunderstorms.[1]

When Captain Ryland returned to the orderly room, her first sergeant informed her that Wichita Falls was under a tornado watch. It didn't register in her mind as an imminent threat. She was more concerned with the piles of discharge paperwork filling her in-basket. She often stayed late at the office to complete paperwork after the training day was over.

A super-cell thunderstorm had formed north of Abilene and was moving northeast toward Wichita Falls. A fast jet stream five miles above ground level provided further lift and a tilting factor that aided severe storm formation.[2]

Rachel became aware of rain pelting down outside. She realized that parade practice had left her more fatigued than usual so she decided to leave with the rest of her staff. As she walked to her reserved parking space behind the squadron, the gusty wind and driving rain soaked her uniform. She strapped herself into the Bronco and started off base. Sirens went off warning that a tornado had been spotted southwest of the city. Her heart instantly kicked up its pace. Adrenaline poured through her system as she headed down the highway for home. The sky was a peculiar yellowish green. The wind was making it hard to keep the vehicle on the road. She could barely see through the windshield.

Rachel white-knuckled the steering wheel as if she were holding on to a bucking bronco—then she realized it *was* a bucking Bronco. How could she come up with a pun at a time like this? Rachel's mouth was so dry she felt her lips cracking.

She headed east down Route 281 as the mile-wide tornado packing winds over 165 miles per hour leveled Memorial Stadium. The sirens continued to wail above what sounded like a giant freight train. She crossed Southwest Parkway as the monster chewed up the Wichita National Bank a few miles away. Poor visibility had slowed traffic to thirty miles per hour on a road where normal speed was fifty-five. Instead of the usual twenty minutes it took to drive home, it was taking twice that.

As she pulled into the driveway still shaking from the adrenaline surge, she clicked open the garage door with the remote expecting to see Bob's Corvette. The garage was empty. Where was he?

The cold panic she had kept at bay on the drive home seized her. He was out in the middle of the tornado somewhere! "Oh, God," she prayed, "let him be safe. Send your warrior angels to protect him!"

Inside the house she got out of her wet uniform, still stiff from the drive, and put on a terry cloth robe. Where were the dogs? She found Charlie under the bed and Rascal in a corner of the walk-in closet. They were shaking uncontrollably and wouldn't move from their hiding places.

"Poor things," she cooed. "You must be petrified." Listening to the radio she learned that the tornado had passed and was heading north toward Oklahoma. Rachel realized if she had delayed her departure for even twenty minutes she would have been traveling down Route 281 just as the tornado crossed the highway. But where was her husband?

Bob had been shopping at Sikes Center Mall when the tornado approached. It was suicide to stay inside the mall but just as dangerous on the road. Bob thought Rachel was probably still at the squadron. She would be safe inside the brick structure if the storm passed over the base.

As he ran for the Corvette, stabbing pain struck his spine. It had only been a few months since his surgery. If he could get away from the mall, maybe he could find a place to pull off the road and hide in a ditch. The sky was completely black. All he could hear was the devouring wind bearing mercilessly down upon him.

Just before arriving at the turnoff for Route 281, he drove onto the shoulder of the road next to a culvert. The wind was so powerful that when he opened the door it was nearly ripped off its hinges. Struggling around the car against the wind, he dove into the culvert. He flattened his body against the concrete covering his head with his arms to protect himself from flying debris. Any minute he expected to hear the Corvette thrown around like a toy. He only hoped it wouldn't land on top of him. Then suddenly all was quiet. The twister had passed by.

The next day the newspaper reported forty-two fatalities. More than half of those were vehicle related. People who had attempted to outrun the storm were blown off the road and killed.[3] Miraculously, Bob wasn't one of them. He was unhurt except for bruises and abrasions. When he climbed out of the culvert he was stunned to find his Corvette sitting right where he'd left it.

CHAPTER 13
Aftermath

THE BASE WAS IMMEDIATELY MOBILIZED to provide disaster relief. Personnel with any kind of a truck were asked to help families retrieve their property from devastated areas. Captain Ryland loaded four airmen from her squadron into a pickup truck borrowed from the base motor pool. For two days they ferried household goods from one part of the city to another. Many families were temporarily staying with friends in areas not affected by the storm. It was incredible to see miles of residential and commercial areas leveled to the ground. Again and again people were heard to remark, "It looks like a war zone." In some neighborhoods homes on one side of the road were destroyed while those on the other side were completely intact, leaving the owners with survivor guilt.

The Sunday after the tornado, Rachel and Bob learned that members of a nearby Baptist church had begun choir practice when the sirens went off. They took refuge under the strongest-looking archway of the vestibule. The church was completely destroyed except for the archway where they were gathered. Minutes after they left the structure, the archway also collapsed.

Another story told of a young mother who was fleeing from the mall with her three-month-old baby. The baby was torn from her arms by the wind. The woman was admitted to the hospital in shock with her arms frozen in position. Days later the baby was found in Oklahoma. It was assumed that it had been carried there by the tornado. Hard to believe, but somehow it had survived without a scratch, and it was returned to its mother.

Everyone seemed to know of similar miraculous incidents. For days squadron personnel could talk about nothing else. It was the most destructive tornado in Texas history, but thanks to excellent early warnings, it was not the deadliest.

The airman showed great satisfaction at their part in the relief effort. Morale had never been higher. Many unforeseen blessings were concealed in the devastating wind. A spirit of brotherhood and selflessness characterized much of the relief effort. It was also evident in Bob's attitude toward his own adversity. After his miraculous escape, he began attending Sunday Mass with Rachel. He also joined a men's Bible study group. His depression and anger disappeared. No longer was he focused on his own suffering but was attentive to the needs of others.

A few months after the tornado Bob applied and was accepted to Stanford Law School. Rachel was alerted that her next assignment would be Hickam AFB, Hawaii. Bob flew out to San Francisco. He stayed with his younger brother, Harmon, and his wife, Connie, while he looked for an apartment to rent near the Stanford campus.

The brothers had been close growing up but seldom had the chance to spend time together since Bob entered the Air Force. Harm was two years younger and had graduated from Stanford with a degree in journalism. He'd escaped the draft because of extreme near-sightedness. He was an introvert and preferred to stand on the sidelines and observe rather than be at the center of action like his brother. Except for his glasses and his shorter stature, his features bore a strong resemblance to Bob's. After working for a small paper in Washington, D.C., for two years, he returned to California to work for the *San Francisco Chronicle*.

Harm was interviewing the mayor of San Francisco about the Chinatown renovation when he met Connie, who was working as a city planner. Her obvious competence and enthusiasm were a strong attraction. She was also a striking-looking brunette. She was slender and wore becoming but understated business suits. She actually resemembled Rachel in physical appearance.

Connie fell in love with Harm's Mr. Magoo charm and they were married within a year. Although she enjoyed her job, when their first child was born Connie elected to stop working. It was a willing sacrifice. A year later she became pregnant again. The two boys were now six and eight. She planned to go back to work when the children were older. Their home was always a beehive of activity with Connie at the center of it. The furniture was carefully selected to withstand the onslaught of two small boys but managed to look elegant when the couple entertained. Harm always said Connie was a frustrated interior decorator.

"It's going to be great having you so close by for a change," Harm remarked to his brother over the delicious chicken cacciatore Connie had prepared.

"I can't believe how fast your boys are growing. They were babies the last time I saw them," Bob said.

"We look forward to being your extended family, especially since you and Rachel will be separated while she's in Hawaii," Connie added.

"She plans to fly back on military hops as often as possible," Bob said. "It's only about 1,500 miles away. There are daily flights between Hickam and Travis. While I'm in law school she plans to complete Air Command and Staff College by seminar during her off-duty time. I'm hoping we'll both be too busy to mind the separation too much."

"That sounds like a plan," Harm replied. "Have you figured out where you'll practice law when you graduate?"

"It will depend on where Rachel's stationed. She'll be coming up on twenty at that point. We're going to play it by ear until then."

"There are so many unknowns, aren't there?" Connie added.

"We're trusting God to lead us. Ever since the crash we've been learning to live one day at a time. Sometimes it is hard not to get caught up in worries about the future, but God has a way of humbling us whenever we think we've got life all figured out."

"We can relate to that, can't we, Connie?" Harm said.

After finding an apartment in Palo Alto, Bob returned to Wichita Falls to pack up the household goods he would be transporting separately from Rachel's overseas shipment.

Shortly before her tour ended, Rachel's group commander, Colonel Kaufman, called her into his office.

"Take a seat, Captain, I have some news for you," the colonel said as she sat at attention in front of his desk. She knew immediately her orders had been changed and drew a quick breath.

"Is this good news or bad news, Colonel?" "A little bit of both. Would you like the good news first?"

"Yes, sir."

"I just returned from sitting on the promotion board for major. It's off the record, but I thought you'd like to know you've been promoted." The colonel leaned back in his executive desk chair to watch her take that in.

"Thank you, sir," Rachel replied, feeling stunned. "I completely forgot the board was meeting already. With all the work getting ready to hand the squadron over and arrange for my move, I wasn't even thinking about it. That really is good news. What's the bad news, sir?"

"The bad news is, since you've been promoted, the commander of PACAF wants to send you to Yokota to be part of the Fifth Air Force planning staff. I think someone up there knows you."

"That wouldn't by any chance be Major General Vandenberg, would it, sir?"

"You guessed it. With your background in planning for the admission of women cadets, I guess he figured you'd be a natural at strategic planning as well."

"I'm going to Japan instead of Hawaii? That's more than twice the distance. It'll be a little harder to see my husband in California. It's still going to be a three-year tour, isn't it, sir?"

"Yes. I know you were counting on Hickam, but you'll just have to take longer hops. Yokota is a major air terminal. You should have lots of opportunities to get back to California. I'm sure you'll manage."

"Yes, sir."

"I think you'll find the assignment very challenging. You'll be working with the Japanese Self-Defense Force as well as the South Koreans. Sometimes things that seem like bad news actually turn out to be the best thing that could have happened."

"Thank you for your encouragement, Colonel." Rachel left the office feeling frustrated and depressed in spite of the news of her promotion.

Rachel thought how pleased her father would be for her. Although she was frequently in touch with her parents by phone she hadn't seen them since before she and Bob were married. Living in Westchester County, New York, they'd been too far away for a visit. Her mother had been working as a fundraising director for a home for emotionally disturbed boys. Since his Air Force retirement, her father had been chief of security for a manufacturing company. They had recently retired to San Antonio and were going to take care of the two dogs while Rachel was overseas. They drove up to Wichita Falls to collect the animals.

"How goes it?" the colonel said as he emerged from the car and shook hands with his son-in-law. He was well over six feet and still wore his silver hair in a military buzz cut. In spite of painful osteoarthritis, he managed to convey an aura of well-being.

"We're doing well, Colonel. How was the drive?" Bob asked.

"Made it in a little less than six hours," the colonel said, pleased with himself.

"I'm so glad you're here!" Rachel said as she embraced her mother and then her dad. At sixty-five her mother was still a beauty. She wore her dark brown hair in a smooth French twist. She was about Rachel's height with the same athletic build. When Rachel was growing up, it delighted her when her mother's friends would say she looked just like her.

The dogs were kicking up a storm in the backyard, wanting to investigate the newcomers. "I'd better let them in or they'll be coming through the screen door," Bob said.

Charlie and Rascal came bounding into the living room. "Oh, what a pair you are!" Rachel's mother cried in delight as she ruffled their coats. "We're going to enjoy having you with us."

"We'll miss them a lot, but we're so grateful you can take them," Bob said. "It wouldn't be practical to take them overseas, and I won't be around too much while I'm in law school."

"We are very happy to have them," the colonel said. "Now that we're both retired they'll get plenty of attention."

"Let's sit down and I'll get some drinks," Rachel said. "The guest bedroom's all ready. It's great to have you here."

Bob took care of the luggage stowing it in the guest bedroom. After everyone was settled with their beverage of choice—scotch for the colonel and his daughter, iced tea for the others—Rachel shared the good news she had just received from her group commander. Everyone was pleased with her promotion, but no one was surprised except Rachel. The colonel reached into his shirt pocket and fished out something gold and shiny.

"I thought you might like to have these," he said, holding out a pair of gold oak leaves that he'd worn during World War II.

"Oh, Dad! How did you know?"

"I just took the chance that you might have news by now." He gave one oak leaf to Bob and together they pinned them on her shoulders. Rachel grinned at her mother, whose smile was equally radiant. Tears sparkled in her eyes. Her father rubbed the side of his nose, an old trick to hide the tears that were threatening to trickle down his face.

Pulling herself together Rachel said, "That's the good news. Now for the bad news. Because of my promotion PACAF wants me to go to Yokota to be on the planning staff at Fifth Air Force."

"That's over five thousand miles from San Francisco," Bob stated, well aware of the distance because he had once aspired to fly the Far Eastern route for United.

"I'm afraid so," Rachel said. "Even though there are plenty of flights from Yokota to Travis, the travel time is three times as long."

"You are both young and strong," her mother interjected, always an optimist. "You'll find a way to see each other despite the distance."

The following day Rachel gave her parents a tour of the squadron and the aircraft hangar where her students were learning to maintain various types of aircraft. It was obvious that they were both extremely proud of her. On the drive back to the house the colonel remarked on how impressed he was with the looks of her squadron and the obvious respect the airmen showed her. After dinner Bob and the colonel had a chance to talk.

"We're so glad to hear you decided to go to law school. You should do well," the colonel remarked. "You know my father went to Stanford."

"I didn't know that, sir."

"He graduated in 1896, Phi Beta Kappa," the colonel added with obvious pride but trying to downplay it.

"He must have been among the first undergraduates. The school was only founded in 1885," Bob said. He knew this from his brother, Harm, who was a history buff.

"My father went to work for a British importing and exporting company in San Francisco and eventually went to Japan to open a station in Kobe. My mother went to work for him as his secretary when he was right out of Stanford."

"Rachel has mentioned that you were born in Kobe. It must have been a very different sort of childhood for you."

"Yes. I grew up speaking Japanese and English with equal fluency. Before the first World War five thousand Europeans were living in Japan. Almost half of them were British, a third were American, and the remainder were German. My younger brother and I were sent to boarding school in Andover, Massachusetts during the war. That's the reason I ended up at Princeton instead of Stanford."

Rachel and her mother joined the two men in the living room after cleaning up in the kitchen.

"One thing that's nice about my reassignment is that I'll be able to see where you were born, Dad. I've always thought it was so romantic that Granny went to work for Grandfather in the 1890s and ended up living in Japan. It must have given her parents a fit when she took a job so far away from home. She had a lot of courage."

"Courage born of love," the colonel said. "She was not only courageous but beautiful and intelligent as well," he added.

"That's why you married Mom, right, Dad? Courageous, beautiful, and intelligent?" Rachel said.

"I fell in love with her the moment I saw her singing in a musical review for the benefit of the Lighthouse for the Blind in Chicago," he said.

"That was in 1931 just after I'd graduated from college and was singing with the Chicago Opera Company."

"Tell us about your parents, Bob," the colonel prompted.

"My parents were both Scandinavian and lived in a small Minnesota farming community. My brother and I were raised there in the '50s."

"Your parents obviously gave you some good, solid Midwestern values. Living close to the soil gives you an appreciation for what's important," the colonel observed.

"They taught us love of family, love of country, and the value of hard work," Bob said.

The evening continued to be a pleasant one. Bob charmed them and he in turn was warmed by them. His own parents were deceased, having been killed in a car accident when he was at the Academy.

The next morning the dogs climbed into the back of the Buick, tails wagging furiously, eager for a ride. Rachel and Bob were left alone in the driveway, feeling forlorn.

"They'll be good company for my folks and they'll love them like crazy, but I'll sure miss them," Rachel said, watching the Buick disappear down the dusty road.

"You know we're not just *loaning* them the dogs, right?" Bob said with his arm around her waist.

"Yes. No chance my parents will be able to give them back after three years."

"When we get settled down again maybe we'll adopt some more," Bob said.

CHAPTER 14
Yokota AB

RACHEL WAS UNPACKING BOXES IN her quarters at Yokota when she got a long-distance call from her older sister. They didn't speak often so Rachel was surprised to hear from her. "I've got great news!" she announced. "I'm pregnant!"

"How wonderful!" Rachel replied. "Now Mom and Dad will finally have a grandchild, and I'll be an aunt!"

"Yeah!"

"How far along are you?"

"Two months. We figure I'll be due to download in May."

"I'm so pleased for you. What did Mom and Dad say?"

"They're thrilled. I don't think they thought I'd ever have a kid since I waited until I was almost forty."

Rachel recalled how silent her parents had been when she told them about her hysterectomy. She realized that her sister had never mentioned it either. She figured it probably didn't even register with her. It never occurred to Rachel that her sister might have been gloating over the fact that she alone had produced their parents' first grandchild.

After hanging up from the long distance phone call Rachel tried to visualize her sister pregnant and immediately thought of the new Air Force pregnancy uniforms. She never thought she'd see the day when women were allowed to be pregnant on active duty.

The next day she went to the clothing sales store and purchased a pregnancy uniform in her sister's size. The uniform consisted of a dark blue sleeveless smock worn over a uniform blouse. The skirt and pants looked the same as a standard uniform with the exception of a pregnancy panel.

She imagined her sister wearing it with different-colored turtlenecks. No one would know she was wearing an Air Force uniform. But Rachel would know and it made her feel like she was sharing the experience. As she paid the cashier she thought how ironic it would be if her purchase started a rumor that *she* was pregnant. Women officers were always hot gossip.

Rachel was fully aware that by sending her sister the uniform she was vicariously fulfilling her own desire to have a child. She and Bob had stopped talking about adopting. It never seemed practical. It was even less so now that they were separated by thousands of miles for three years. She called Bob to tell him of her sister's news, then quickly changed the subject.

"How do you like law school so far?"

"I think I'm really going to like it."

"What are the other students like?"

"I haven't really gotten to know anyone. Most of them are ten years younger than I am."

"How are Harm and Connie?" Rachel asked.

"They're doing well. Connie's working part-time at a friend's antique shop and the boys are busy with soccer. I'll be spending Thanksgiving with them. I wish you could join us."

"I do too. I'll be lucky to get a hop over the Christmas holidays. Maybe I should just book a commercial flight instead."

"Not a bad idea. Why don't you check on the rates? If you book this far in advance I'll bet you can get a good fare."

"I'll see what I can do. I'll write you what I find out. Thank goodness for the GI bill. If we had to pay for your Stanford tuition, this long-distance commuting would break us."

"Take care of yourself. I love you, babe."

"You too," Rachel choked out.

While she was processing in to the base, Rachel ran into an old friend from Randolph. Colonel Ann Curwen had been chief of protocol for Air Training Command. They met during a base tennis tournament, became good friends, and played tennis almost every weekend.

Ann had been married to a fellow officer who was stationed at the Military Personnel Center at Randolph. Ann had been miserably unhappy. She finally divorced him just before being sent to Thailand as the Vietnam War was winding down.

Although they hadn't seen each other for years, the two women officers picked up their friendship right where it had left off.

"It seems just like old times, doesn't it?" Ann said as they walked onto the tennis courts behind Fifth Air Force Headquarters.

"Yes, it does. I haven't had a steady tennis partner since Randolph, though. I'm afraid I'm a bit rusty." Rachel had played on the varsity tennis team in college. Ann had been the ATC singles champion three years in a row.

They hit the ball back and forth until Rachel began to feel her swing getting back in the groove. It was a crisp fall day and the cool breeze made it a pleasure to be outside. They wore traditional white tennis dresses. Both were tall and slender. Ann wore her long blond hair in a bun with a coronet of braid. On some women it may have looked old-fashioned. On Ann it looked regal. Rachel had never seen her friend wear her hair any other way in uniform or out. Rachel's short dark hair was cut in a flattering wedge made popular by the Olympic skater, Dorothy Hamill.

"Are you ready to play a game?" Ann asked. "Sure."

They played three sets. Ann's strength was consistency. She never made an unforced error.

Rachel had a pounding serve that was usually accurate. She had a nice spin on her forehand and a reliable backhand. They had always been evenly matched, but somehow Ann always won two out of three sets. Deep down Rachel didn't think it was good form to beat an opponent who outranked her.

When they finished playing, Ann invited Rachel to her quarters for a cold drink. They talked for an hour. Rachel revealed how concerned she was that her career would wind up ending her marriage. Ann's own experience was testimony that it was hard to combine marriage and a career especially in the military.

"I just found out that my older sister is pregnant. I think she called me from Boston just to rub my nose in it. I never really grieved the loss of my ability to have children. It's like my biological clock never got the message to stop ticking. Do you regret that you and Neal didn't have children?"

"In a way I do," Ann admitted. "But with Neal's alcoholism I worried that a child would inherit a predisposition. Neal didn't want children anyway and he was so emotionally unavailable he wouldn't have been a good father. Once we were divorced I was grateful that we didn't have children. Combining a military career with motherhood is hard enough. Being a single parent on active duty is almost impossible."

"It must have been so difficult living with an alcoholic. I knew you were unhappy but didn't realize alcoholism was a factor. You never said anything while we were at Randolph."

"Like most people married to alcoholics, I was ashamed."

"What gave you the courage to divorce him?" Rachel asked.

"I realized that I wasn't helping him. In fact, I was hurting him by staying in the marriage. The rescuer in me was as much addicted to the dysfunctional relationship as he was addicted to alcohol."

"Were you afraid to be single again?"

"Yes. You know how it is in this all-male environment. You're fair game even when you're married. I was very vulnerable for a while."

"That's how I feel now. I'll be separated from Bob for three years."

"I divorced Neal just before my remote tour to Thailand. I was single for the first time in ten years. While I was there I had an affair with Colonel McLaughlin . I'm sure you remember him. He was the Director of Information at Randolph."

"Of course. I always thought he was good looking but a little on the short side."

"He and his wife were getting divorced, so I guess it was kind of inevitable that we would seek each other's company while we were on a remote tour."

"Didn't people gossip?"

"We were very discreet. But, yes, everyone knew we were seeing each other. It isn't unusual for people to have affairs overseas. It would be more unusual if they didn't. Being separated by thousands of miles of ocean makes it seem safe."

"You're really making me worry now."

"It's probably different for you and Bob, you being Catholic and all. You have the church for support."

"You make it sound like a crutch."

"I don't mean to. I always envied your faith. Even though I was reared an Episcopalian I don't go to church anymore. I sometimes long for the kind of spiritual relationship you seem to have with God."

"Why don't you come to our prayer group sometime? We meet every Wednesday night at the chapel. We're just about to begin a Life in the Spirit seminar. It's about how to have a personal relationship with God through the Holy Spirit."

"I'll think about it. Remind me again next week, okay?"

The conversation turned to more mundane topics like shopping trips to the Ginza in downtown Tokyo. They made plans to take the train into town for some early Christmas shopping during the upcoming Columbus Day weekend.

CHAPTER 15
Catherine

BOB WAS COMING OUT OF the law library when he almost knocked over another student. She was carrying a load of books that fell from her arms. After much mutual embarrassment, Bob asked if he could buy her lunch by way of apology. She accepted.

Over lunch they discovered they were both in their first year of law school. Catherine was newly divorced and had one child. Her parents lived in San Francisco and were helping look after her seven-year-old daughter. Bob explained where Rachel was and that they were planning to be together over Christmas.

"It's good she can fly back to the states now and then," Catherine said while toying with a chef's salad.

"I'm looking forward to seeing her," Bob replied, all the while thinking it was rather nice to be talking to this attractive young woman who shared his interest in the law. She was medium height with light brown shoulder-length hair and eyes the color of topaz. She had a reserve about her that played well into his natural gregariousness.

"Why did you decide to go to law school?" she asked.

"I've always needed a sense of mission. After serving in the Air Force for eight years I became an airline pilot. An accident caused me to stop flying. I wanted to do something with my life that would make people's lives better. I'm hoping that as a lawyer I can do that. What about you?"

"My father's a lawyer. I've always wanted to study law, but I got married right after graduating from Stanford and then Beth came along."

"So you were a Stanford undergraduate as well," Bob mused. "My younger brother was class of '69. What year did you graduate?"

"I was class of '70. But my ex-husband was class of '69. Maybe they knew each other. What was your brother's major?"

"Journalism."

"Richard was political science, so I guess their paths never crossed."

"Probably not, but it's an interesting coincidence." Bob made a mental note to ask Harm about Richard the next time they talked.

Their lunch was cut short by the need to get to their afternoon classes. Catherine thanked Bob for lunch and they hurried off in separate directions. She thought what an interesting guy he was and hoped maybe they could be friends. Bob thought the same thing about Catherine.

The following weekend Bob had dinner with Harm and his family. He told them about meeting Catherine. Harm did, in fact, remember Richard Richardson.

"He was all about power. Had big political ambitions. I think he went to Washington to work for a senator. I'll bet he was a horror as a husband."

"I didn't get into that with her," Bob said.

"She sounds like an interesting person. Do you plan to introduce her to Rachel when she comes home for Christmas?" Harm asked with barely perceptible sarcasm.

"I haven't thought about it," Bob replied a little too quickly.

"Okay, you two," Connie said deftly, changing the subject. "The boys have a soccer game and Uncle Bob is coming along." She hustled them all into the family van.

Richard Richardson did go to Washington. After a one-year internship he returned to work in the California senator's San Francisco office. He picked up his relationship with Catherine where they'd left it after his graduation. With dark hair and eyes he had the kind of craggy good looks that stopped just short of being handsome. He exuded a menacing power to his enemies and frequently lost control of his hair-trigger temper with his coworkers.

He could be charismatic when he wanted something, and he wanted Catherine. She was impressed with his Washington sophistication. Richard was working his way deeper into the San Francisco political machine when they were married.

In spite of her excellent Stanford education, Richard devalued her intelligence. He preferred to keep her as a political appendage. Pregnancy brought on high blood pressure, which forced her to stay out of graduate school or the job market. Instead she focused on the arrival of their child. Richard was disappointed it was a girl. He started pressuring her to get pregnant again to produce the wanted boy. Catherine was reluctant due to the blood pressure problem.

In spite of Richard's criticism she enjoyed being a new mother, and her parents were delighted with their first grandchild. Catherine confided to her mother that Richard wanted her to have another child immediately. Her parents were appalled that their daughter could fall in love with a man who was so self-centered. They didn't criticize him in front of her but they worried.

As time went on Catherine became pregnant again, but at three months she miscarried. Richard had a fit. His ego was so tied to his ability to produce a male heir that he had no concern for his wife's health. Catherine developed panic attacks. She was not only afraid of becoming pregnant; she was afraid of Richard. He kept her under his thumb, and she felt trapped.

One night he came home from work after having a few drinks with his political cronies. Two-year-old Beth was asleep in the nursery. After entering the living room he grabbed Catherine's arm and kissed her roughly. She pulled away. The smell of liquor on his breath nauseated her. It wasn't the first time he'd come home drunk. She tried to distract him.

"You must be hungry. I saved your dinner in the oven. Why don't I warm it up for you?"

"I'm hungry all right but not for dinner." He followed her into the kitchen and pulled her to him again. "Come on, baby, let's get another bun in the oven, huh?"

Catherine's heart was racing. She knew if she resisted he would only become more abusive. Maybe he was so drunk he would just pass out if she acted like she would cooperate.

"Why don't you go on into the bedroom and get comfortable while I just check on Beth. I'll be right in," she offered. This time her stalling tactic worked. But several nights later he wasn't put off so easily. He raped her.

Catherine knew she was going to have to get away from him before his violence escalated, but she also knew he wouldn't let her go.

CHAPTER 16
Team Spirit

EVERY SPRING FIFTH AIR FORCE participated in a joint military exercise with forces from Japan and South Korea called Team Spirit. Colonel Maldonado, Major Ryland's boss, gave her the exercise plan to review. It was voluminous. As she studied the document she learned how the exercise had evolved.

Team Spirit was born in 1975 during a time of political controversy. It consolidated several smaller exercises, conducted since 1969, into a comprehensive field maneuver with both military and political objectives.

Although Team Spirit was billed as completely defensive, the North Koreans always contended it was preparation for an invasion. This assumption was not surprising as prior to their invasion of South Korea in 1950, the North Koreans used military maneuvers to mask troop movements.

The exercise involved 156,700 South Korean and U.S. Army, Navy, and Air Force personnel. It was U.S. Pacific Command's largest exercise.[1]

For one month forces were deployed to the Korean Peninsula. Major Ryland observed the exercise with other members of the planning staff and gathered after action reports from the field that she consolidated into a report on the overall effectiveness of the logistical support, which included coordination of supply, maintenance, and transportation.

Each member of the planning staff had their designated area of expertise: air operations, logistics, and personnel. The other staff officers privately referred to Colonel Maldonado as "Waldo Not Know" because they viewed him as someone who had been promoted to his level of incompetence.

The colonel was a former transport pilot who had flown two tours in Vietnam. His Air Medals testified to his excellence as a pilot. He was short in stature and exhibited the sensuality often associated with Italian men. He enjoyed good food, good wine and beautiful women. His wife of twenty-six years divorced him while he was in Japan. He was thought to be a womanizer, but that was only speculation. He had salt and pepper gray hair and the Mediterranean complexion that testified to his Italian heritage.

Like most pilots who were no longer flying, he detested paperwork. For this reason he delegated all of the details to his staff and didn't seem to take much interest in how well they completed their work. On the upside he more or less left them alone. He was due to retire in another year.

Major Ryland tried not to notice the way he seemed to fixate on the rows of ribbons beneath her jump wings on the left side of her chest. She told herself he was just reading her awards, but the musing expression on his face always made her uncomfortable.

One Saturday, after playing tennis with Colonel Curwen, she expressed her concern about her boss.

"Has he ever made a direct pass at you?" Ann asked.

"No, but he's probably getting ready to."

"We all have our share of sexual harassment, you know," Ann reminded her.

"I know. It's part of the job. Maybe because I came out of an all-female environment I feel more threatened. I should've learned how to handle this in college. I keep forgetting that I'm not seen as a co-professional by most of the men but rather as a target. I had a really frightening experience while I was at the Academy."

"What happened?"

"It was after the Navy football game. Bob and I were at a party at the quarters of the Navy liaison officer. It was getting late.

Almost everyone was downstairs in the finished basement. There was a lot of noise and smoke. I had a headache so I went upstairs to sit quietly in the living room while Bob stayed downstairs talking to my boss. Three officers from my department were sitting at the kitchen bar. I didn't say anything to them. They were talking loudly and it sounded like they were drunk. One of them was Major Evans, who always making suggestive remarks at the office. He said to the others, loud enough so I would hear, 'Let's all go rape Rachel.' I didn't think he was serious, but I was alarmed.

"He came weaving over to where I was sitting on the couch, leered into my face, and said, 'If we didn't like you we wouldn't kid you.'

"I said, 'If you were my friend you wouldn't kid about something like that.'

"He suddenly turned on me and started calling me every name in the book. He accused me of being a tease and said they were all sick and tired of it. At that point I really felt threatened. I went downstairs and got Bob and told him we needed to go home. He was standing right next to my boss. Bob asked me what was wrong. I didn't want to tell him what had happened. He wouldn't let it go. I finally had to tell him what Major Evans had said. He wanted to go up there and punch him out. Colonel Hill told him to take me home and he would handle it."

"How did that go?"

"The next morning the colonel called Major Evans into his office and read him the riot act. As you can imagine, from then on I was shunned by the men in my department. Most of them took Major Evans' side. I don't know how I could've handled the situation differently. The only thing that made it bearable was shortly after that I was appointed chief of the Special Planning Staff and my office was located in another building."

"I know it's a cliché, but it's a case of damned if you do, damned if you don't," Ann said. "Just by your existence you represent a threat to the male ego. If you're very good at your job, and I know you are, you're a professional threat. If you're attractive, and you are, you're a sexual threat. It doesn't matter how carefully you conduct yourself. All of the men will be wondering what you're like in bed. They resent you simply because you're there and unobtainable."

"Sometimes I wonder if it's even worth it to try to stay in," Rachel said.

"You've just made the first big hurdle by being promoted to major. There is no question that it's an uphill battle. I can tell you right now that it's only going to get harder. But the fact is you've already invested twelve years of your life. Why not stick around for at least eight more? With your record I think it's a pretty safe bet you'll make full colonel. Even if you don't you can retire at twenty and not lose your benefits."

"I know you're right. Everything seems so much harder being separated from Bob. I guess I just need time to adjust. I'm going to spend Christmas with him in Hawaii. I'm really looking forward to that. Bob's always been so supportive of my career, and I feel guilty that I'm not there to support him while he's in law school."

"Doesn't he have a brother who lives close by?"

"Yes, thank goodness."

"I'm sure your letters and calls mean a lot to him. He's a big boy. He'll get through law school just fine. He's an Academy graduate, isn't he?"

"Yes, and he's extremely bright. Things are going fine for now. I guess I project too much into the future. I'll be starting the Air Command and Staff seminar soon. Staying focused on my work and school should keep me too busy to brood about things."

"That a girl! See you next Saturday for our regular game. In the meantime you can always call me if anything gets out of hand."

"Thanks. I will."

CHAPTER 17
Assault

CATHERINE RICHARDSON WAS VULNERABLE AND she knew it. She was immediately drawn to Bob Ryland. He was attractive and kind. She sensed that he had been deeply hurt by events in his past. Perhaps they had that in common. She had strict rules about dating married men. She didn't do it. But wasn't having coffee after classes harmless? She knew better and vowed she wouldn't encourage his friendship. She even went out of her way to avoid him. But she couldn't help thinking about him. The holidays were coming up and that helped her to keep her mind focused on her seven-year-old daughter, Beth. Catherine was grateful that her daughter had a sunny disposition and an inquiring mind. Beth was tall for her age and on the skinny side. Her hair was caramel-colored and worn in long braids which Catherine delighted in ornamenting with colorful ribbons.

One day in December they were Christmas shopping at a mall in Palo Alto when she spotted Bob in Macy's with a statuesque brunette. Catherine assumed this was Bob's wife, Rachel. They made a stunning couple, and she went home feeling depressed.

Beth provided a momentary distraction. She immediately wanted to help her mother with gift wrapping. Even though she was tired, Catherine indulged her daughter.

"Will Daddy be home for Christmas?" Beth asked while tying a bow.

I hope not, Catherine thought to herself, but she said, "I don't think so, honey. You know how busy he is in Washington. But I'm sure he'll send you a really nice present." This seemed to satisfy Beth for the moment. She was still too young to understand about divorce. Catherine hoped to be able to prevent Beth from being emotionally damaged by her father's rejection. Even though Richard pretended to love Beth, Catherine knew her ex-husband was incapable of loving anyone but himself.

Catherine thought back to past holidays when she and Richard were still married. More often than not Richard was drunk from Christmas Eve until New Year's Day. Fortunately, Beth was too young to realize it. It was their tradition to have Christmas dinner with Catherine's parents. She lived in fear that Richard would do something embarrassing. They had no idea how abusive he was. Catherine was too ashamed to tell anyone. It wasn't until the night his violence put her in the hospital that her secret was out.

It was a Friday night. He had come home intoxicated. Catherine had already put Beth to bed. It was almost midnight. She'd fallen asleep on the couch in front of the television. She felt someone tugging at her in the dark. It was Richard. Although she was half asleep she could smell the liquor on his breath.

"Richard, what are you doing?"

"Teaching you a lesson." He straddled her on the couch.

"Please, Richard, it's late." She tried to push him away, but he smashed his fist into her face. She felt the cartilage in her nose break. She screamed as she rolled off the couch. Beth awoke crying.

Catherine staggered to her feet thinking to go to her daughter. A second blow to the side of her head sent stars dancing through her brain. The room seemed very bright and distant. Something slammed into her abdomen, driving the breath from her and she fell. The last thing she remembered was his foot aimed at her like a torpedo.

When she regained consciousness she felt something touching her face. It was soft and cold, ice in a cloth. It hurt, but the ice was soothing. Her face felt hot and swollen. Worse was the burning deep within her. Yet somehow the pain seemed far away. Slowly she understood she was in the hospital. Then she remembered why she was there. She slept. When she awoke she was in terrible pain. The nurse gave her a shot. Later, the doctor explained to her that she had a ruptured spleen and they'd operated.

After moving back in with her parents, Catherine spent two years in counseling with a therapist who specialized in battered women. She still attended a therapy group and found it helped her deal with the lingering nightmares and depression. One of the reasons she wanted to become a lawyer was to empower other women victims. This was not something she shared with her fellow law students as to disclose her personal history still filled her with shame.

CHAPTER 18
Christmas

DECEMBER SEEMED TO FLY BY. On Christmas Eve Catherine and Beth were planning to attend a children's service at 6 p.m. As Catherine slipped a black velvet jacket over her red knit dress, the doorbell rang. Her parents were out attending a social function. Beth was still in her room. In a hurry to get to church, Catherine was irritated by the interruption and opened the door without checking through the peephole to see who was there. Richard stood under the porch light holding a poinsettia in one hand and a Christmas present in the other.

"Oh, my God!" Catherine croaked as she took in the shock physically.

"Merry Christmas! Did I surprise you?" He laughed, wickedly self-satisfied. "Aren't you going to invite me in? I want to see my little girl." Catherine knew his unexpected visit had nothing to do with his desire to see Beth. She felt her throat starting to close with anxiety.

"We were just on our way to Christmas Eve service. Beth is singing in the children's choir. You could come with us, I guess." Catherine shuddered at the thought, but she knew Richard would insist on joining them anyway. Beth ran into the hall to see who was there.

"Daddy! Daddy! You came! You came!" Beth cried.

"There's my favorite girl!" Richard gushed, scooping her up like the doting father he wasn't.

Catherine wondered what his real agenda was.

"Is that for me, Daddy?" Beth asked, eyeing the present. "Can I open it now?"

"We'll save it for later. We don't want to be late for church," Catherine said firmly.

"Are you coming with us, Daddy? I'm singing in the children's choir!"

"I'll bet you're the best one!"

"We really should leave now," Catherine said. "I'll put the present here on the hall table."

The last thing Catherine wanted was to arrive at the Presbyterian Church with her ex-husband.

Over controlling as always, he insisted on taking his rental car, which he had deliberately parked in the driveway to block Catherine's exit. When they got to the church Beth ran to the choir room to get into her robe with the rest of the children.

Catherine and Richard found a place near the back of the already crowded sanctuary. The organist was playing a medley of old English Christmas carols. Evergreen wreaths with red satin bows adorned the side walls, giving off a piney scent. A tall Christmas tree decorated with white twinkle lights stood on one side of the altar. The congregation murmured around her.

Catherine kept her nose in the program, which had been handed to her by one of the ushers. Sitting next to her abusive ex-husband made her skin crawl. Her mind was racing like an engine with a slipped clutch. Why is he here? He wants something. How can I get rid of him and not upset Beth?

These thoughts were interrupted by the opening chords of the processional hymn. The congregation stood as the children, ranging from age four to nine, processed down the aisle. They were achingly cute in their royal blue cassocks and white surplices. Beth was toward the back with the older, taller children. Catherine tried to catch Beth's eye as she passed, but her daughter's focus was riveted on Richard.

The service lasted about one hour. Catherine was eager to collect Beth and get away from the church before anyone could ask who her tall, dark escort was. She had not shared her story with anyone from church and wasn't about to start on Christmas Eve, if ever.

"How about a stop at the pancake house?" Richard asked, knowing Catherine could not deny her daughter this treat. It was safer to go to the restaurant than to be alone with him.

After they ordered, Catherine asked her ex-husband what had brought him to San Francisco. He gave the excuse of political business for his senator, but she knew he really came to check up on her.

CHAPTER 19
Hawaii

CATHERINE WAS MISTAKEN ABOUT WHO it was she saw with Bob at the mall. It was actually his sister-in-law, Connie. Rachel was still in Japan. The day before Christmas Rachel caught a military hop to Hickam. They had decided to meet in Hawaii as it was midway between their two homes. The sun winked off the long flat waves of Waikiki as the C-141 Starlifter banked into a final turn on approach to Hickam airfield. Bob had already landed on the commercial side of the airfield, which shared runways with the base. He was at the air terminal in a rental car to pick her up. They stayed in the Visiting Officers Quarters to avoid the expensive, overbooked hotels in Honolulu.

After checking in to their room they dropped their bags and stood in a long embrace. They were wrapped in each other's arms for the next two hours as they made urgent love to each other.

At dinner Bob was full of enthusiasm for his law classes and Rachel shared stories about the office, although she didn't reveal her concerns about Colonel Maldonado.

"I knew you'd do well in law school, honey."

"It's like I have a sense of mission again, you know?"

"I do know," Rachel said.

"Have I told you how much I love you in the last hour?"

"I can always hear it again. Do you think we'll be able to get through the next three years?" Rachel asked.

"Let's not think of it in terms of years. Let's take it a day at a time."

The day after Christmas they checked out snorkeling equipment from Recreational Services on base and headed off for a day of exploring. Bob drove a rented Mustang convertible. The wind blew Rachel's short curls around her head. Bob wore a Stanford ball cap and pilot's sunglasses.

Their destination was Hanauma Bay, located on the back side of Diamond Head. The bay floor is actually the collapsed crater of an ancient volcano. The curvature of the bay protects it from large ocean waves and provides a perfect environment for snorkeling. The coral reefs extend a mile out and provide a stunning habitat for a dizzy variety of tropical fish.

After a day of snorkeling and sunbathing, they returned to the base for a quiet dinner at the Officers' Club. Bob looked relaxed and tanned in a safari shirt and pants, eschewing the gaudiness of a Hawaiian print. Rachel wore a long, black, polished cotton dress with a printed white hibiscus trailing down one side. A dramatic off-center slit showed off her toned legs. She wore a lavender orchid in her dark hair, which gave her an exotic appearance.

"You are very beautiful tonight," Bob said. "But I always forget, which side do you wear the flower on if you're married?"

"I don't remember either. Afraid someone might make a pass at me?"

"They'd better not."

"And you look like an adventurer in your safari shirt."

"Anytime I'm with you is an adventure," Bob remarked with a small smile. Rachel thought how true that was on both sides.

"What shall we do tomorrow?" she asked.

"I thought we'd go for a hike around Waimea Falls."

"I've heard they're great to swim under."

"It'll take all morning to drive around to the north side of the island, but I think it'll be worth it," Bob said.

"It might get us away from the tourists."

When they reached their destination, it took three hours to climb to the top of South Ridge following switchback trails of mud and loose gravel. It was a difficult climb through a forest of exotic native plants, but once on top they had a breathtaking view of the 18,000-acre Waimea Valley.

Before descending they ate sandwiches and fruit that Bob had carried in a day pack. South Ridge is located behind the waterfall. When they completed their descent they were rewarded with a cooling swim in the natural pool at the bottom. The mists rose around them in rainbows. The seclusion of the spot offered a perfect opportunity for the couple to renew their intimacy. Bob put his arms around Rachel's tanned body, pulling her close to his own. The fullness of his desire for her was overwhelming. They didn't wait to return to base before making love.

The days passed too quickly. They were soon parted at Base Operations, where Rachel would board another hop back to Yokota. Bob left to return the rental car and wait for his flight at the commercial terminal. Since she had to travel in uniform on military aircraft, she drew considerable attention in the predominantly male waiting area. Rachel tried to pretend to herself that their parting was only for a few days instead of several months. She hid her turbulent emotions from the prying eyes of the crowded room. Once airborne, Rachel turned her face to the bulkhead and let the tears fall.

CHAPTER 20
Life in the Spirit

W HEN TEAM SPIRIT WAS OVER, the officers on the planning staff settled into a calmer routine.
Although Major Ryland enjoyed the challenge of crisis management during the exercise, it was nice to get back to a normal pace.

Rachel was looking forward to attending a Life in the Spirit seminar sponsored by the Catholic chaplain. Her good friend, Ann Curwen, had agreed to attend with her. Ever since receiving the Baptism of the Holy Spirit at a Full Gospel Businessmen's convention in Montgomery, Alabama, Rachel had a more vital relationship with the Lord. Although her life was not free from anxiety or loneliness, she could always commune with Jesus in her heart. She talked to him as if he were her best friend. She still prayed the Rosary and other Catholic prayers, but she found that praying in the spirit offered a special intimacy. This spiritual communion was hard to put into words, but other "spirit-filled" Christians knew the same experience. Rachel wanted to share this with her friend.

The seminar would last six weeks. Rachel and Ann lived in the same high-rise apartment complex so they met in the lobby. Rachel offered to drive. "Are you ready for this?" she asked as they walked to the parking lot.

"As ready as I'll ever be," Ann replied. "I'm feeling a little nervous."

"That's normal. Once we get there you'll relax. Father Delaney's really special, and I know some of the presenters. I think their experiences will resonate with you."

"Well, I'm just grateful they'll allow a backsliding Episcopalian to join them."

"There will be other non-Catholics there," Rachel said as she started her car. "This is an ecumenical group. You don't have to be Catholic or even Christian to join."

Cherry blossoms exploded everywhere with pink blooms. As they pulled into the parking area light streamed through the windows of the sanctuary like welcoming arms.

Inside the chapel they were greeted by singing. Song sheets were passed out to new arrivals. Many of the words were based on the Psalms. The hymns were easy to follow.

Spirit of the living God, fall fresh on me. Make me, mold me, fill me, use me. Spirit of the living God, fall fresh on me.

Soon Ann's clear soprano blended with Rachel's alto. Many of the participants raised their hands in praise, some waving gently. Rachel imagined she could reach out and touch the face of Jesus.

The subject of the first talk was an overview of the gifts of the Holy Spirit. The presenter was one of the longtime members of the prayer group. She read from 1 Corinthians, Chapter 12:

"But the manifestation of the Spirit is given to each one for the profit of all. For to one is given the word of wisdom through the Spirit, to another the word of knowledge through the same Spirit, to another faith by the same Spirit, to another gifts of healings by the same Spirit, to another the working of miracles, to another prophecy, to another discerning of spirits, to another different kinds of tongues, to another the interpretation of tongues. But one and the same Spirit works all these things, distributing to each one individually as He wills."

"So there you have it. All of the gifts of the spirit: wisdom, knowledge, faith, healing, miracles, prophecy, discernment of spirits, varieties of tongues, and interpretation of tongues. Tonight we'll be discussing the first two gifts: wisdom and knowledge."

The presentation was followed by a question and answer period and more singing. Refreshments were served in the parish hall where people could mingle informally. On the drive back to their quarters on the other side of the base, Ann told Rachel she was impressed by the sincere friendliness of the group.

"I've never felt so accepted and loved by a group of strangers," she said as they crossed the darkened airfield. Blue lights outlining the taxiways cast a peaceful glow that seemed to follow them home.

"It's consoling, isn't it?" Rachel replied, pleased that Ann mirrored some of her own feelings. "You're not nervous anymore, are you?"

"No, I feel such a peace. I'm so glad you asked me to come. I can hardly wait for the next meeting."

"I feel the same way. In the meantime, are we still on for tennis Saturday?"

"You bet. I'll meet you at the court at our usual time," Ann replied.

In spite of her deepening spiritual life Rachel still struggled. She frequently sought Father Delaney's spiritual direction. His wisdom and empathic understanding never failed to encourage her to have faith in the rightness of her calling. He was a stout Irishman with a merry twinkle in his eye. He was in his late fifties and had ministered to members of the Air Force for over twenty years. As a full colonel he was the head chaplain at Yokota. He was serious whenever counseling one of his flock, but he always injected humor into his homilies. The week after the seminar Rachel made an appointment to talk about her long term marital separation. She always felt at home in the chaplain's office. It was comfortably furnished with a sofa and arm chairs in addition to the standard office furniture. There were shelves of books lining two sides of the office containing Bible commentaries, papal encyclicals and various theological tomes. There was a huge rubber plant in the corner by the sofa. The leaves were shiney from being polished regularly by the chaplain's assistant who showed Rachel in. Father Delaney got up from behind his desk and extended his hand in greeting. Rachel took his hand and was then enveloped in a friendly hug.

"Top o' the mornin' to ya!" he said with his best Irish brogue. He offered her coffee or tea and then led her to the sofa. After a little small talk about the Life in the Spirit seminar Rachel got down to business.

"Father, how can I know if I'm in God's will?"

"God engineers our circumstances so that we will follow his plan for our lives even when it doesn't seem clear what that plan is."

"I feel like I'm wandering in the wilderness. I'm thousands of miles from my husband, who is courageously embarking on a new career. Instead of being by his side I'm pursuing my own achievements. Isn't that self-centered and egotistical?"

"Maybe Bob needs this time alone to grow closer to Christ. Sometimes in a marriage dependence on each other can crowd out the need for dependence on God."

"Yes, I can see that. Maybe the separation is part of God's plan so that both of us can become closer to him. I guess deep down I'm really worried that Bob will find someone else."

"Life is a series of tests. If your relationship with Bob is as strong as I think it is, you'll both resist the temptation to be unfaithful."

"I guess I just need to stay close to Jesus."

"That's exactly right." Father Delaney said with a pat on her shoulder and a twinkle in his eye. As she left his office the burden of false guilt fell away.

CHAPTER 21
Richard

TWO YEARS AFTER HIS CHRISTMAS visit, Richard returned to San Francisco to run the reelection campaign for his senator. He called Catherine repeatedly to ask her out on a date, leaving dozens of messages on her answering machine. She steadfastly ignored them. When he showed up on campus a couple of times she began to get nervous.

One Saturday night Catherine was alone, preparing for an important exam. Her parents were on a cruise to Alaska. Beth was spending the night with a friend. The startling sound of the doorbell violated the silence of the house. Catherine padded to the door. As she squinted through the security peephole a wave of nausea hit her. She took a slow, deep breath to gather her courage.

"Go away, Richard. I don't want to see you. We're divorced, remember?"

"That was five years ago, Catherine. I'm a different man now. Just give me a chance. I still love you. I've never stopped loving you."

"If you don't leave I'm calling the police."

"Don't be like that Cathy. I just want to talk to you."

"Go away. I mean it," Rachel shouted through the door. Richard backed away, but he had no intention of being put off so easily. Catherine peaked out the living room window to watch him drive away. Two years of counseling after he had brutally beat her had taught her that men like Richard don't change.

When he started stalking her she bought a .38 caliber revolver for home security. Bob Ryland took her to the firing range to teach her how to use it. By this time she had confided the story of her marriage and divorce to him.

After Richard left she called Bob. "He's gone now, but I'm so rattled. I would've called the police, but I don't have a restraining order so there's not much they can do."

"You should definitely *get* a restraining order. He has been stalking you. That should be enough to get one. Do you have your .38 handy in case he comes back?"

"Yes, I do. Thank goodness Beth is spending the night with a friend."

"Do you think he'll come back?"

"He might."

"Do you want me to come over?"

"No. I'll be okay. But thanks. I feel better now that I've talked to you."

"Well, call me if you change your mind."

"I will. Good night, Bob."

Just after midnight a car without headlights on crept down the street and stopped at the curb just beyond Catherine's driveway. It sat there like a panther waiting for its prey. A shadow detached itself from the still form and crept around behind the darkened house. As if guided by some primitive instinct, the shadow found an unlocked window and slithered in.

Catherine had just put aside her books and turned off the light by her bed. Sensing something alien in the house, she was instantly alert. Without turning on the light she carefully got her .38 out of the drawer of her night table. She listened tensely for a sound. In her gut she knew it was Richard. She felt pinned to the bed like a dead moth.

"Is that you, Richard?" Her throat was raw with fear. No answer. She sat up straight and held the .38 in the two-handed grip Bob had taught her. She forced herself not to hyperventilate so her hands would stop shaking. The night-light from her daughter's bedroom revealed a shadow moving silently toward Catherine's open bedroom door.

"What do you want?" she cried.

The shadow spoke. "I want to know what you're doing with a married man whose wife is stationed overseas with the Air Force."

It didn't surprise her that he knew this information, but she didn't answer. His icy calm accusations were always a prelude to a sudden escalation of violence.

"I've been watching you with him on campus. It seems like you're quite close friends." She remained silent, although she was aching to defend her friendship with Bob.

Richard remained crouched in the hallway silhouetted by the low light. Catherine held her breath. Suddenly he sprang into the room toward the bed where she sat rigid with fear. "I guess I'll have to teach you another lesson, won't I?"

Remembering the last time he said those words, Catherine fired a shot. It went wide. "What do you think you're doing, you little bitch?!" He lunged toward her to grab the gun. Reflexively, she fired again. This time at such close range the bullet found its mark. Richard fell to the floor. Appalled by what she had done, she dropped the pistol as if it would burn her. Her next-door neighbor heard the shots and called the police.

When the squad car arrived minutes later she was going into shock. After questioning her for over an hour, they took her into custody. She was charged with murder. After the arraignment, she was released on bail. When the police technicians had processed the crime scene, Catherine returned to her parents' house. Beth had been staying at a friend's house until her return.

Because of who Richard worked for, the shooting made the national news. Bob read about it the next day and called the house. He left a message on the answering machine.

"Catherine, I'm so sorry I didn't come over last night even though you told me not to. Please call me. I want to do what I can to help."

When Catherine played her messages, she realized that everyone in her law school class knew about the incident, but Bob's call was the only one she returned.

"My parents have hired the best criminal attorney in San Francisco. I'm out on bail. The trial probably won't be set for another six months. In the meantime, I'm dropping out of law school."

"Maybe when this is all cleared up you'll be able to return. It was self-defense, right?"

"Yes, but I'll have a hard time convincing a jury that I was in fear for my life. He didn't have a weapon. I thought he was going to attack me like he did the last time."

"Surely that will come out at the trial. How is Beth taking all this?"

"She doesn't understand what happened. She's upset and angry. We're both going to counseling. My parents will take care of Beth if I have to go to prison."

"Don't give up on your attorney. I can't believe that you won't get off."

CHAPTER 22
Seoul

COLONEL MALDONADO CALLED MAJOR RYLAND in to his office to inform her of his plan to have her accompany him on a trip to Seoul. "Next month is the tri-service conference at Yongsan Army Garrison ," Colonel Maldonado began. "In addition to our Army and Navy staff officers there will representatives from the South Korean Air Force and the Japanese Self-Defense Force. I want you along to take notes and observe. The exposure will be good for you."

Major Ryland thought to herself, *Exposure to what?* But she replied simply, "Yes, sir."

Rachel had already met a few South Korean officers along with Japanese officers who were on liaison duty at Fifth Air Force. She always enjoyed engaging them. They were courteous and professional. She wished her male counterparts were as respectful.

"I want you to contact Lieutenant Liu at Yongsan," Colonel Maldonado continued. "He's the South Korean representative coordinating our itinerary. His contact information is on this letter from his headquarters. We'll be staying at the Visiting Officers Quarters, of course. Be sure to reserve adjoining rooms."

Rachel felt the first frisson of apprehension.

She didn't like the idea of being quartered so close to him. She wished others from her office would be attending the conference to give her a buffer.

Yongsan garrison was originally created as a Japanese garrison in 1910 when the Empire of Japan annexed Korea. It was then located on the outskirts of Seoul on mostly undeveloped land. By the 1980s the city had grown to completely envelop the garrison.

It was considered a perk to go to Seoul as clothes could be custom-made there for a song.

Her friend, Ann Curwen, briefed Rachel on where to have a uniform made.

"I have already bought enough material for a jacket, skirt, and pants," Rachel said. "That's the upside of the trip. The downside is we'll be alone together. I just know he's going to try something. How can I avoid an embarrassing situation? I don't really dislike the man. I want to be respectful but keep my distance."

"The most important thing to remember is don't drink. If you do, don't have more than one."

"You're right. Alcohol always loosens my tongue. I'm bound to start talking about how much I miss Bob, and the colonel will think that's a come-on."

"Since it is only a two-day conference you only have to worry about one night. You can probably avoid having dinner with him without being impolite. If he knocks on your door later in the evening just don't let him in. Whatever his ploy may be, you can always work around it."

"I hope so."

The Sunday before her trip to Yongsan, Rachel spent several minutes after Mass pondering her situation. Separated from her husband by thousands of miles of ocean, they no longer shared a life together. Long-distance phone calls and letters seemed dismally inadequate. When they met in Hawaii once or twice a year, the time was much too short and Rachel felt worse when they parted.

Looking up at the crucifix, she begged for an answer. *Is this what you really want me to do? I'm not sure I even want to do it anymore. Why am I doing this?* Repressed grief over her childlessness also insinuated itself into these quiet moments.

As he was passing through the sanctuary, Father Delaney noticed Rachel. He gently touched her shoulder and said, "Is there anything I can do?"

"Oh, hi, Father. It's the same old dilemma. What means more to me, my marriage or my career?"

"Maybe you don't have to make a choice. It's not necessarily all or nothing," Father Delany said as he sat down in the pew.

"I'm just afraid my marriage will slip away from me if I don't take decisive action."

"How does your husband feel about it?" Father Delaney asked.

"He's so busy with law school I don't think our separation bothers him as much. He seems to be able to compartmentalize better than I can."

"I know you've prayed about this for a long time. Sometimes we can overanalyze the cross we have to bear. God doesn't expect us to be objective about our suffering. It is not up to us to determine if we're doing it right. We can't look inside our own soul to see if God's work is being accomplished. All God asks of us is to embrace our daily duties and leave the big picture to him."

"Sometimes I can do that, but underneath there's anxiety and doubt."

"And you know the cure for that, don't you?"

"Yes, Father. Trust."

"The more a soul trusts the more grace it will receive," Father Delaney said.

"I'll try to remember that, Father," Rachel replied as she stood to leave.

The flight to Incheon International Airport was under two hours. Their arrival time was well before the first scheduled activity. A staff car from the garrison met the plane and carried them to the VOQ. The conference began with a welcome luncheon followed by small group meetings focused on various aspects of the plans for the bed-down of forces and logistical support in the event of an invasion of South Korea.

Rachel found the meetings enlightening. She took detailed notes and gathered papers provided by the briefing officers. Much to her surprise, Colonel Maldonado was completely professional. He didn't ask her to dinner or try to ply her with drinks after the business of the day. It occurred to Rachel that he might have a female friend in Seoul whom he planned to visit. She felt silly to have built up such apprehension.

Free from any dinner commitments she had plenty of time to visit the Korean tailor. All she had to do was leave her uniform and they would copy the pattern exactly. When she picked up the finished product the next day it was almost like magic. The workmanship was superb. The fit was perfect and the price was incredible.

During the second day of the conference at Yongsan, Major Ryland became better acquainted with the Japanese Self Defense Force officer with whom she'd worked at Yokota. Captain Kitazama told her a strange story.

One day while walking home from school, his twelve-year-old sister, Noriko, was kidnapped by a man believed to be a North Korean.

"When did this happen?" Major Ryland asked.

"Two years ago," Kitazama replied.

"Why hasn't your government been able to get her back?"

"Hundreds of Japanese citizens have been abducted."

"Do you know why is this happening?"

"From intelligence reports we believe some have been abducted to teach the Japanese language and culture at a North Korean spy school. Older ones were abducted to steal their identities; they were probably killed right away. Some were abducted to be wives of North Korean-based Japanese terrorists. Most women were in their twenties."[1]

"Why would they take a twelve-year-old schoolgirl?"

"My family lives in Niigata on the northwest coast. We think she accidentally witnessed some illegal activity of a North Korean spy."

"What do you think has happened to her?"

"They say she committed suicide, but I don't believe she's dead. Her body has never been found. She was always a very bright girl and had a gift for languages even at such a young age. I think she was probably forced to marry a North Korean spy."

"How terrible for you and your family. Isn't there an ongoing investigation?"

"Not really. The North Koreans deny everything, of course. My government only acknowledges a few cases. They are afraid to incur the wrath of the North Koreans. The other missing persons have been written off as a disappearance, not abduction. My sister's case was never investigated by the local police because they consider her a runaway."

"Do you think you'll ever see her again?"

"I pray so. My parents will not stop urging the government to pursue the matter."

"Is there anything the U.S. government can do?"

"No. Not now anyway," Kitazama replied with resignation.

Major Ryland vowed to keep the story in the back of her mind, and if she ever got the chance she would see what could be done by the United States to help Japanese families locate their missing relatives in North Korea.

CHAPTER 23
A Healing

ON THE RETURN FLIGHT, COLONEL Maldonado seemed relaxed and even talked about his children, who were with his ex-wife in Virginia.

"How old are they?" Rachel asked.

"My daughter is fourteen and my son is a senior in high school. He's the star quarterback on the football team, and he's just been accepted to attend the Air Force Academy."

"Following in his father's footsteps, I see."

"I really miss not being able to go to high school football games to watch him play."

Rachel heard the pain in his voice. She felt a pang of empathy. She realized they had a common bond. They were both separated from someone they loved. It hadn't occurred to her before. She made a mental note to add him to her prayer list.

Father Delaney was right about trust, she thought. She no longer felt defensive and resolved never to allow fears of sexual harassment bother her again.

While in Seoul Rachel was only a few blocks away from the world-renowned Full Gospel Church of Pastor David Yungi Cho.

In 1981 the church had a membership of 400,000. Rachel had read about Pastor Cho's powerful evangelistic services in a Christian magazine. When he came to Japan on a mission some months later, she invited Ann Curwen to join her for a Friday night service at a large Assembly of God church in Tokyo. They took the train with several other people from Yokota.

Pastor Cho preached on the power of forgiveness and how it relates to physical and emotional healing. After his sermon people were praying and singing in tongues. On the train back to base Ann told Rachel what she'd experienced.

"I asked God to help me to forgive my ex-husband for all the pain he has caused me. As I was praying silently with my eyes closed I felt the hands of others on my shoulders and heard them speaking gently in a language I'd never heard before. The emotional pain of my marriage slipped away like an unwanted, worn-out garment. The singing and praying was so comforting. I felt like I was standing in a gentle rain while the sun was shining."

"I'm so glad we had this opportunity," Rachel said. "I actually saw his church while I was in Seoul, but of course I didn't have the chance to hear him preach until tonight."

"You know how Pastor Cho said you don't have to *feel* forgiving to make it an act of will?" Ann asked.

"Yes. I sometimes let my anger get in the way of my prayers because I don't feel like praying. I have to make it an act of will, and once I start praying the anger goes away. I may not get the answers I'm looking for, but I feel better just by being faithful to my prayer life."

"I didn't expect anything to happen, but when I felt people's hands on my shoulders and heard them praying in tongues I knew that God was answering my prayer," Ann said. "Even with my eyes closed the whole room seemed brighter. I suddenly felt lighter. It was like I was being carried. Do you know what I mean?"

"I do know. When I first received the baptism of the Holy Spirit with the gift of tongues, I felt the same way. I've always liked that verse from Deuteronomy: "The eternal God is your refuge and underneath are the everlasting arms.""

"I am so glad I attended the Life in the Spirit seminar with your Catholic prayer group," Ann said. "It prepared me for this moment. I'd like to start going to Mass with you. I might even ask Father Delaney if I could receive instruction to join the Church."

"We can make that happen," Rachel said.

CHAPTER 24
Lake Shoji

THE AIR COMMAND AND STAFF seminar at Yokota provided an opportunity for Rachel to meet officers outside her headquarters. One of these was Captain Tom McCaffrey. He was a UH-1 helicopter pilot assigned to the airlift wing. He flew medivac missions and ferried VIPs around the mainland. He was average height with dark hair and eyes. He was known for his practical jokes.

Rachel found him refreshing. He also rode a candy apple red Yamaha. The bike was his most prized possession. His wife drove a Honda station wagon more suited to hauling their three kids around base. On weekends she rarely saw Tom as he was usually off on a ride up to the mountains or down to Yokosuka to visit naval aviator buddies from the aircraft carrier *Enterprise* when it was in port.

Rachel had ridden a motorcycle once in 1963 while she was at Wellesley. She had a blind date for the Dartmouth-Harvard game. Her older sister, then a junior at Radcliffe, invited her to come for the weekend. Her date rode a motorcycle and she was introduced to the thrill of hugging a complete stranger to and from the football stadium in the pouring rain. In spite of the rain she was thrilled with the ride.

Unfortunately, she developed a bacterial infection in both eyes and had to go to the emergency room at Massachusetts General Hospital for treatment. She wound up wearing patches over both eyes. Her temporary blindness was a metaphor for what everyone felt that weekend. President Kennedy had just been shot. It seemed the whole country was temporarily blinded by grief.

When Tom asked if she'd like to join him on a ride to Lake Shoji, she jumped at the chance. After the two-hour ride they would tour the ice caves at Narusawa and then return to base.

Rachel was very familiar with the region as she'd heard about it from her grandmother. As an agent for a British importing and exporting company, her grandfather was the station manager in Kobe. Her grandmother was originally from a logging town in Humboldt Bay. She took a secretarial course in San Francisco before being hired by her future husband. Their courtship began almost immediately. When he was transferred to Kobe he asked her to marry him.

Rachel's ride on the back of a Yamaha was tame compared to the trip her grandmother made in 1904 in the midst of a typhoon. Rachel had the letter her grandmother had written to her mother describing her honeymoon trip to Lake Shoji.

Mother Dear,

You will be glad to know your lass arrived safely in Yokohama Harbor. Hal came out to meet me on the first launch. Shortly after landing we were married by the American consul and the Episcopal bishop from Tokyo. You see, we were married tightly enough to satisfy even you.

We went to the Imperial Hotel in Tokyo for lunch and a brief rest before boarding the Tokaido line to Gotemba, a city on the southeastern flank of Fujiyama. Hal hired a special horse drawn tram for the next leg of the journey. Actually it was a cart drawn by a shaggy little pony. It looked like a toy. A coolie, clad in blue cotton shirt and pants with a blue and white towel around his brow, bowed us into the tram. We wedged ourselves into seats about a foot wide on either side of the cart. Our bags were loaded in the middle where the driver normally sat. The little coolie ran alongside driving the pony. I noticed a bamboo flute hanging from his girdle along with a pipe and tobacco pouch. I wondered if he would serenade us later.

After five cramped hours in the little sidecars we began the ascent of Mount Fuji on a single narrow track. Just as we were about to get out of the tram, the air was broken by a weird musical crescendo. Almost immediately a reply came from our driver's flute. He pulled the pony to an abrupt halt and motioned frantically for us to get out. "Hyaku! Hyaku!" he shouted, which meant "quickly."

We complied without question although it was no easy task. With no wasted motion the driver unhitched the pony and shoved the ram off the track just in time for a descending tram to pass, the passengers blissfully confident of their right-of-way. This ritual continued all the way to the top of the mountain. Finally we reached a little inn where we spent the night.

The next morning we began the second leg of our journey. We had to take a kago, or bamboo chair, slung upon a long pole with a coolie at each end. Twelve men and two kagos had been sent from Shoji to carry us to the lake.

We started out unaware that the barometric pressure had been falling steadily. Oblivious to the impending bad weather, we enjoyed the picturesque scenery, peerless Fuji dominating every view. About four o'clock in the afternoon we arrived at Lake Shoji where we were to be met by a launch to carry us across the lake. The skies had become overcast and the wind was already chopping the water. The old man at the dock told us we could not put out across the lake as the water was already too rough. There was nothing to do but keep on in the kagos and go around the lake, a journey of about twelve miles. We were only a short distance into the forest when the storm broke in all its fury. The rain came down in torrents. Lightning strikes felled trees across the narrow path. Even with the protection of the coolies the high wind caused us to be thrown out of the path into the rocks. We were forced to abandon the kagos and continued through the storm on foot.

After three hours of trekking in this manner we arrived at the inn soaked to the skin but unhurt thanks to the care of our coolies. For the remainder of our trip the weather was gorgeous as it always is after a typhoon, which seems to cleanse the skies.[1]

Of the five lakes in the area around the foot of Mount Fuji, Shoji is the smallest. It is situated 2,951 feet above sea level. In 864, Mount Nagayama, a volcano that flanks Mount Fuji, erupted. Lava flow spread across the area, damming up rivers and resulting in the formation of the lakes. They remain connected by underground waterways. As the outer lava gradually cooled and shrank, gases and molten lava inside flowed out, carving out a cave inside the formation.

Rainwater and snow-melt from Mount Fuji permeate the volcanic rock. As a result, water drips constantly inside the caves. The temperature averages thirty-two degrees Fahrenheit year-round.[2]

Tom had visited the ice caves once before but wanted to make a second trip to photograph the incredible scenery.

"In the winter stalactites hang down from the ceiling about three feet," he told Rachel, playing tour guide. "The water dripping from the ceiling freezes and forms stalagmites, which grow upward. Sometimes the stalactites meet the stalagmites, creating continuous ice pillars that extend half a mile underground."

"Sounds like a fairyland," Rachel said. "Too bad you can't get your wife to go. I guess your kids are too young."

"Yes. It would be pretty tricky for toddlers to navigate. The cave floor is covered by a pond of perpetual ice more than nine feet thick. The path is protected by wooden planks."

"It does sound a bit treacherous," Rachel said. The two-hour ride along Route 139 was breathtaking for Rachel, and not only for the scenery. Tom rode with great expertise and confidence. She was enjoying the sensuous pleasure of hugging his well-toned abdomen, but as they passed other motorists around blind turns, she had to close her eyes and say a few Hail Marys. She couldn't help but think of the perilous journey her grandmother had made in the little pony cart.

When they arrived at the inn on Lake Shoji she was treated to a spectacular unobstructed view of Mount Fuji. Tom dug out their down parkas and ski caps from the saddlebags, replacing the leather jackets they had worn on the ride. Rachel fancied their chic ski bum appearance. Two hours later she didn't feel quite so chic when they emerged from the caves. Some of the passages were so low they had to squirm through on their bellies.

At the end of the icy half-mile journey Rachel remarked, "I must say, I'm really glad the sun is shining today." They were both shaking with cold in spite of their warm clothing.

"It's a good thing we're making this trip in September," Tom said. "It's pretty rough to go through these caves in the winter."

"Let's get back to the inn. I want to spend the rest of the afternoon in the hot tub."

Later they found they were too tired to make the two-hour ride back to Yokota. They decided to spend the night at the inn. As it turned out the inn was booked solid. The desk clerk could only offer them a single room. Fully confident that Tom would be a perfect gentleman and not eager to contemplate another hair-raising ride on the Yamaha, especially in the dark, Rachel accepted the accommodations.

When they got to their room she was in for a surprise. Unlike in the states where even single motel rooms have more than one bed, their room was equipped with only a lonely queen. Tom handled the situation gracefully by offering to sleep on the floor. However, when she awoke the next morning she wasn't alone. Her nose was cold, but the rest of her was toasty warm. *Where was she?* Then she remembered. Oh, yes. Lake Shoji. What happened last night? Whatever it was she felt delicious. Wait a minute, she realized she was snuggled into a man, one arm resting across his chest, and her face nestled into his shoulder.

There was a moment of panic and then horrified realization. She opened one eye and exclaimed, "Oh, God."

"No, just brother Tom," her motorcycle partner said.

"Sorry, I must have mistaken you for Bob."

"No need to apologize—nothing happened."

"Are you sure? After that delicious dinner and bottle of Saki I don't remember the rest of the evening," Rachel admitted with chagrin.

He chuckled at her consternation. "I'm going to take a shower," he said, slipping out from the warm covers. Rachel turned to the other side of the bed in case he was the type who slept in the raw. He was such a practical joker he probably did just to freak her out.

Rachel decided to forgo a shower and slid into her flannel-lined L.L Bean jeans and a turtleneck sweater for the ride home. She was contemplating a hearty breakfast when Tom emerged from the bathroom wrapped in a small white towel, which he barely held together across his hunky torso. She tried not to stare, but it was impossible to drag her eyes away.

"Uh, I think I'll go on down to the dining room while you get dressed," she said as her face turned bright red.

"Why? Do you think you'll be tempted to ravage my irresistible masculine body?"

"Something like that." She scurried out the door and down the stairs to the dining room. It was still very early. Rachel sat by a picture window looking out on the lake, which was shrouded in an exquisite purple haze. Then it turned to a rosy gold. Then the sun seemed to fairly leap into the sky, revealing Fujiyama in all its pure white, snow-capped beauty. It reminded her of the early morning ski trip to Aspen. Pike's Peak had been pinked by the sun that morning too. She longed to be back there with Bob.

CHAPTER 25
Earthquake

RACHEL FINISHED HER TOUR AT Yokota just in time to attend Bob's law school graduation. She sat with his brother, Harm, and his wife, Connie. As she watched Bob accept his diploma, Rachel felt their mutual sacrifice had been worth it.

Her next assignment was to Travis AFB. It was only an hour from Oakland, where Bob would begin his law career as a public defender. They settled into a house in Vallejo, halfway between their two workplaces.

Bob chose to become a defense attorney as a result of the murder trial of his former classmate, Catherine Richardson. Although it was ruled self-defense, she was convicted of manslaughter and sentenced to ten years in prison. It raised Bob's awareness of the predicament of battered women.

After three years as a staff officer at Fifth Air Force, Major Ryland was glad to return to the nuts and bolts of base-level maintenance. Her squadron maintained the C-5 Galaxy and C-141 Starlifter. Both aircraft played a vital role in maintaining the balance of power in the world.

During her tour at Travis, the wing supported several important troop deployments to Central America. They were part of U.S. efforts to counter Nicaraguan incursions into Honduras, and they played a role in the toppling of Panamanian dictator Manuel Noriega.[1]

Rachel and Bob spent much of their off-duty time with Harm and Connie and their two teenage boys. During his law school years Harm became close to his nephews.

The boys were avid baseball fans. They particularly enjoyed attending baseball games at Candlestick Park. When their favorite team, the San Francisco Giants, made the World Series in 1989 the boys were ecstatic.

Just before the third game of the series, Bob called his brother from the Alameda County Courthouse. "Glad I caught you before you left. I'm tied up at the courthouse for a while so I'm going to be a little late. I'll meet you in our seats, okay?"

"Sure, Bob, no problem."

"How're the boys?"

"Excited. But Sandy's come down with a sore throat so he's staying home with Connie."

"That's a shame. I'm sure Connie will take good care of him. At least he'll be able to watch it on TV. I'll see you as soon as I can get there."

"Okay, buddy."

Harm and his older boy, Will, hopped in the car and headed for Candlestick Park. They lived in suburban Sunnyvale, which was about an hour away.

It was a warm and breezy day, perfect Indian summer weather for the game. Harm and Will took their seats in plenty of time to watch batting practice. Then a loud rumbling shook the stadium.

"What was that, Dad?" Will asked.

"It sounds like rolling thunder," Harm replied. Then the stadium shuddered. Light towers swayed. The foul-line poles in left and right field whipped back and forth. Although expansion joints at the top of the stadium absorbed the impact of the earthquake, chunks of concrete fell off.[2] One block crashed into Section 53 right next to where Harm and Will were sitting.

Harm's wife, Connie, was watching the game on TV with Sandy. The picture began to jiggle, then went black.

"Aw, what the heck!" Sandy exclaimed. "Why do we have to have a power failure right at the start of the game?!"

"Wait a minute! Connie screamed. "The house is shaking!" She was pinned to her recliner in terror. The movement rolled Sandy off the couch and onto the floor.

"*Mom! Are we going to die*?!"

Connie threw herself out of the recliner. "Get under the dining room table with me, NOW!" she ordered.

Bob was approaching the Oakland Bay Bridge on the top deck of I-880 when the earthquake struck. Due to the warm weather he had the top down on his 1979 red Corvette. He gripped the steering wheel as the car bounced up and down. It felt like a really bad landing in his F-105, but flying a fighter in combat was not nearly as frightening as keeping his car on the road at that moment. A fifty-foot piece of roadway broke off and fell on to the lower deck, carrying him and the Corvette with it.

Bob knew immediately what was happening. "Sweet Jesus!" he cried. As the car fell he was sure he was going to die, but something caught him just in time. He slowly realized that he had landed on top of other cars on the lower deck. In despair he thought of the people crushed beneath him.

As he sat pinned in his crumpled car, he felt blood trickling down his scalp. Shards of windshield glass littered the front seat. He managed to unbuckle his seatbelt. Then a stabbing pain hit his spine. His mind flashed back to the crash of United Flight 173 when he'd been similarly wedged into the cockpit of the DC-8 he was flying as first officer to Portland, Oregon. Then everything went black.

CHAPTER 26
Rescue

MAJOR RYLAND WAS NOT THINKING about baseball. She knew Bob was going to the game with Harm so she took the opportunity to work late. One of the C-5s the squadron was working on was down for parts. She called the maintenance support section, irate over the delay.

"Well, when do you think you'll have them?"

"Oops," replied the supply officer, as his in-basket slipped to the floor. Gripping the phone in one hand and the arm of his shaking desk chair in the other he asked, "Did you feel that?"

"You bet your bippee! Looks like a big one. Better get out now!" She dropped the phone, grabbed her purse, and made a hasty exit from the hangar along with her maintenance personnel. After about fifteen seconds the shaking stopped. It didn't appear that there was any danger to her people or the airplanes.

Her mind refocused on the whereabouts of her husband. Was he still at the courthouse, or would he be at Candlestick Park by now? She jumped into her 1974 Bronco and headed for their home in Vallejo. Both she and Bob had CB radios in their vehicles. Thinking Bob may not have made it to the ballpark yet, she tried to raise him on the CB. Using the call sign for his 1979 Corvette, she keyed the mic and said, "Flight 79, this is Flight 74. Can you copy?" Nothing but static. She tried again. Still no response. Well, good. Maybe he's already at the park. Her cramped insides told her he could also be on the Oakland Bay Bridge. When she got home she turned on the television and was glued to the scenes of the disaster.

Connie and Sandy were lucky. The house had not suffered any structural damage. Books had been thrown from their shelves and some glassware and dishes had rattled out of cabinets, but the roof was intact. They huddled together in front of the TV, hoping to get news of the disaster.

The 58,000 spectators in Candlestick Park were at first confused. Then there were screams. When the noise and shaking reached their peak, the spectators fell silent. After it finally stopped the relieved crowd broke into a cheer.

"That's San Francisco," a visitor said with admiration. "They cheer an earthquake!"

Sixteen-year-old Will Ryland yelled, "That was nothing. Wait till you see the Giants bat!"

Since the public address system was out, police used bullhorns to tell the fans there would be no game and they should move slowly to the exits.[1] As Will and Harm made their way from the stadium they saw an ominous plume of black smoke rising into the sky from the northwest.

"That's coming from Oakland," Harm said. "Oh no, Dad! Do you think Uncle Bob was on the bridge?" Will asked, full of dreadful imaginings.

"I hope not, Son. Let's get home to check on your mom and Sandy."

Smoke issued from the crumbling concrete. Beneath the smashed upper deck of I-880, cars had been flattened to the height of six inches. Some of the survivors yelled for help hysterically, others so feebly they could hardly hear their own voices.

Bob Ryland slowly regained consciousness. When he tried to crawl out of the Corvette the stabbing pain in his back returned. He realized he desperately needed help. Turning on his CB radio he flipped the dial to nine, the universal SOS frequency. He thought surely his CB antenna had been damaged by the crash, but he tried anyway.

"Mayday! Mayday! Can anybody copy?" At first there was silence. Then, miraculously, a response came.

"I hear your Mayday! Go ahead," replied a retired fireman monitoring the emergency frequency from his base station.

"My name...is...Bob Ryland," he gasped. "Trapped...I-880... just before...bridge."

"Are you seriously injured?" the fireman asked.

"Don't know... please...call my wife." He gave the number slowly and released the mic.

"Will do. Hang tight."

When Rachel got the call from the fireman she was frantic. Out of reflex she immediately dialed 911, but the lines were overwhelmed. She couldn't bear to sit at home, so she ran back out to the car and began driving toward Oakland. At least she could keep calling Bob on the CB.

She hoped that when she got to the bridge she would somehow be able to help. As she raced past the Mare Island Naval Complex she tried to raise Bob again. No response. Then she realized she was on the frequency they routinely used traveling to and from work. She changed to channel nine, the emergency frequency and called, "Flight 79, this is Flight 74, can you copy?" She repeated the call over and over like a prayer, trying to keep her mind on what Father Delaney had said about trust.

Bob was barely able to hear his wife's call. It took a minute for him to reply. Her voice was like that of a rescuing angel.

"Rach...I...copy," he replied weakly.

Her heart hammered, but she forced herself to remain calm. "I'm headed toward Oakland on the I-80. Traffic is pretty backed up. I'll try to get close enough to tell the rescue crew where you are. Are you badly hurt?"

"Stabbing pain...lower back"

"Don't try to move, honey."

"No problem with that," he replied.

"I'll stay on the CB with you," Rachel said as her vision blurred with tears.

Six hours later the rescue crew reached the Corvette. Bob was in shock. He was immediately airlifted to Alameda County Medical Center. Rachel sat anxiously in the surgery waiting room while he was worked on in the OR. Harm and Connie had arrived and waited with her.

"Did they tell you anything in the ER?" Connie asked.

"He was unconscious while they did X-rays and a CAT scan. It looks like another ruptured disc above his first fusion," Rachel replied, trying to hold back a sob.

"What a nightmare," Connie said.

"I can't believe it's happening all over again," Rachel said. "You know how easily Bob can slip into depression. Just like when all those passengers died in the '78 crash, he'll be feeling guilty about the people who were killed on the lower deck."

Connie put her arms around her sister-in-law and held her as silent tears spilled down their cheeks.

The waiting room was packed with relatives of survivors. Early estimates put the death toll as high as 250. Over three thousand were injured, many seriously.[1]

While the women waited, Harm went to get coffee from the hospital cafeteria on the first floor. As a reporter for the *San Francisco Chronicle*, he had hurriedly scrawled an eyewitness account of what he and Will had experienced at the ballpark. After calling in his story to the paper, he delivered cups of coffee to Connie and Rachel.

Everywhere people yearned for news of what had happened. When a special edition of the paper appeared at 7 a.m. the next day, people threw quarters at sellers and shoved one another to grab a copy.[2]

CHAPTER 27

Decisions

WHEN BOB AWOKE IN THE recovery room, his wife had the chance to see him briefly. Once she assured herself that he was out of danger, she left the hospital. Harm and Connie would be with him and keep her posted until she could return.

Although she'd been up for more than twenty-four hours, Rachel drove straight to the base. She felt grungy as she was still wearing her uniform from the day before. She knew the Air Force would have a vital role to play in the relief efforts. Her place was with her troops.

C-141s maintained by her squadron flew relief equipment and personnel to the South Bay area to assist victims of the earthquake. It was just one of many humanitarian airlift missions they had flown over the years. Rachel was proud of the role her maintenance personnel played in these operations.

Although his recovery from surgery was slow, Bob eventually made a strong comeback. Unlike the period of his convalescence from the airline crash, he did not slip into depression.

He quit the public defender's office and joined a fellow Stanford grad to open a private practice. He loved the challenge of each new case. He was a keen judge of character and could tell when a client was not telling him the whole truth. The truth mattered to him. He would defend a client that he didn't think was innocent because even a guilty client was entitled to a good defense. There were always matters to be considered in mitigation. He was always well prepared for courtroom battles and loved the challenge of having to think on his feet. Other attorneys admired him not only for his superior verbal skills but also for his encyclopedic knowledge of the law. He could argue both sides of every issue, every time. He was soon acknowledged as a rising legal star.

Rachel was promoted to lieutenant colonel and became deputy commander of the Airlift Maintenance Group. During this time the couple made some important decisions.

One night in 1988 after a long duty day, Rachel asked her husband, "You know that old saying 'If the military wanted you to have a wife they would've issued you one?'"

"Are you about to say, 'If the military wanted you to have a husband they would have issued you one'?" Bob replied with a wry grin. He then added, "Does this mean you want a divorce?"

"Very funny. No, I was thinking more along the lines of 'If the military wanted you to have children, etc., etc.'"

"I'll be fifty next year. You're not still thinking of adoption, are you?" he asked.

"No. I just want you to know that I've settled the issue in my mind and heart once and for all."

"Ah," he replied, respecting the gravity of the moment.

"It seems the timing was never right, doesn't it? I've stopped grieving the loss. I guess it was pretty much a closed issue for me when I left Japan. I just never felt ready to acknowledge it."

"It's good to get closure," Bob said.

"With Harm and Connie so close these past few years, I've enjoyed our extended family. We've watched the boys grow up and go to college. I've been very content to be an aunt."

"Plus, you've had your hands full just taking care of me," Bob said with the goofy lopsided grin that she loved.

"Isn't that the truth!" she replied, meaning it.

"You could retire now that you've hit twenty. "What do you think?" Bob asked.

"I still have two more years on my new assignment, but after that I think I'll retire. You're so well established here. I couldn't ask you to relocate."

"Well, actually I've been thinking of making a move," he announced.

"What? What are you talking about?" Rachel asked as her hazel eyes widened.

"I'm thinking of running for the Senate."

"Wow! I'm all for it, but what gave you that idea? You'd be marvelous at drafting legislation and your skills as a communicator would be dynamite on the campaign trail."

"I actually got the idea from an old buddy of mine from Vietnam. We were in the same squadron. You never met him. He's now serving as a congressman from Texas. I happened to run into him at that legal conference I attended last month. He feels the same way I do about how clueless our politicians are about how to run a war. He told me how to put feelers out with our local Republican party. If there is enough interest maybe I have a shot."

"No question. If you run against the current Democrat incumbent you'll wax his tail, to use one of your old fighter pilot expressions."

"I ran the idea by Harm and you know how politically connected he is."

" Yes, he'll be a great asset. He knows how things are done."

Two years later, Bob was elected as a Republican senator from California, defeating the Democrat incumbent.

Rachel was ready to retire and settle down to being a senator's wife. She'd done her duty to the military, and it seemed like a good time to hang up her uniform permanently. Then Saddam Hussein invaded Kuwait and everything changed.

Beginning in August 1990, the 60th Airlift Wing provided airlift and logistics support to U.S. and coalition forces in Southwest Asia while continuing to perform worldwide airlift operations. During Operation DESERT SHIELD and DESERT STORM a total of 1,280 C-5 and 954 C-141 missions were flown from Travis.[1]

Rachel was promoted to colonel, resulting in an assignment to the Pentagon. When Bob was sworn in as a freshman senator, Rachel assumed her new position as Politico-Military Planner, Directorate for Strategic Plans and Policy, Joint Staff, the Pentagon.

Soon after her arrival, Colonel Ryland was notified that she had been selected to attend the National War College. The college is located on Fort Lesley J. McNair in Washington, D.C.

The purpose of the college is to prepare senior officers for higher command and staff positions. Because of its location close to Capitol Hill, the Supreme Court, and the White House, an extraordinary array of speakers is available. The curriculum focuses on the domestic and international contexts in which national security policy is developed. Graduates exercise great influence on the formulation of national and foreign policy in both peace and war.[2]

As their career challenges continued to intensify, the added pressure only made their relationship stronger. They both thrived on pressure. Bob's physical condition was excellent, although he had given up running for walking on a treadmill due to his back surgeries. Rachel continued her running program begun years earlier at the Air Force Academy. However, soon after her assignment to the Pentagon the old parachuting injuries had come back to haunt her. She had been suppressing the pain for years but she could do so no longer. The back injury was the worst because it caused lightening strikes down her right leg. She knew from Bob's experience that her symptoms most likely meant she had a herniated disc in the lumbar region. Small wonder after the beating she took on the 35 foot tower. Her neck pain was localized on the right side running up the ophthalmic nerve and striking her right eye. She finally bowed to the inevitable and went to see a neurosurgeon at Bethesda Naval Medical Center. After a CAT scan revealed two herniated discs in her neck and one ruptured disc at the fifth lumbar vertebrae, she was scheduled for surgery the next day.

It was six weeks before the colonel could return to work. During her convalescence she and her husband had plenty of quality time. Since Bob had undergone disc surgery twice himself he could empathize with her.

Their days were full and as Rachel began to heal their nights were often occupied with social activities. One night, after attending an event at the National Theatre of the Performing Arts, the senator and the colonel settled beside a cozy fire to discuss the coming week.

"The president is meeting with Prime Minister Netanyahu on Tuesday," Bob stated, a vertical line appearing between his brows as his reading glasses slipped down his nose. His blond hair had turned silver, which Rachel thought gave him the look of an elder statesman.

"It probably won't accomplish a thing," his wife replied.

"The president thinks he can negotiate with that terrorist, Arafat," Bob scoffed.

"Netanyahu will take a hard line on troop withdrawals from the West Bank," Rachel observed. "Do you think your committee will have any influence?" The Senate Armed Services Committee was dominated by hawkish Republicans.

"Unfortunately, the president will ignore our recommendations. Secretary Albright is really calling the shots. She'll meet with Netanyahu after the president. She'll do the serious groundwork. Arafat will meet with her the day after. I'm afraid it's a done deal. Netanyahu will be forced to make large territorial concessions."

"How can the president think you can negotiate with terrorists?" Rachel demanded her eyes flashing with anger

"He wants to go down in history as jump-starting the stalled peace talks. He thinks he can pursue a policy of appeasement and you know what Churchill said about that."

"An appeaser is one who feeds the crocodiles in the hope that they will eat him last," Rachel noted.

"We are *not* interested in feeding the crocodiles!" Bob declared.

"Definitely not. Golda Meir must be whirling in her grave. Israel has always depended on us for support. It must seem like a slap in the face for the president to ignore their national security interests."

Bob continued his tirade. "What can you expect? Clinton's foreign policy has been drifting like a downed aviator in a single-man raft for the past six years. He talks tough but doesn't follow through with action."

"With defense spending cut forty percent, we can't back up our allies with action anyway," Rachel said.

"Have you heard the latest story about the first lady?" Bob asked.

"Did she beat Bill up again because of his affair with Monica Lewinsky?"

"No, she beat him up because he won't give her a bigger office."

"She already got the vice president's office."

"Now she wants the Oval Office."

"That's nothing new," Rachel said. "When we were at Wellesley everyone predicted she would be the first woman president."

"That's right. You were in the same graduating class. What was she like then?"

"She was a Republican."

"No kidding?"

"Yep. She was even president of the Young Republicans her freshman year. The civil rights movement and the Vietnam War changed her views. I'll give her this much credit, though, she never advocated the kind of campus demonstrations that took place at a lot of schools in the late '60s."

"We desperately need a Republican in the White House," Bob said.

"You've got that right," Rachel replied.

CHAPTER 28
Yugoslav Wars

I N 1998 PRESIDENT CLINTON FAILED to bring together the Israelis and the Palestinians. At the same time, the Balkan wars presented a far more worrisome problem. Working for the chairman of the Joint Chiefs as a strategic planner, Colonel Ryland studied the history of the wars in Yugoslavia.

When Slobodan Milosevic became president of Serbia 1991, he wanted to dominate all of the old Yugoslavia, which had been divided into six republics. When he found that he couldn't do that he sought a federation dominated by Serbia. The Yugoslav armed forces were largely Serbian. When Slovenia seceded from the federation, hostilities erupted.

In January 1992, a peace plan brokered by the U.S. brought an end to major military operations, but it didn't last. Five months after the end of major military operations, war broke out in Bosnia. To link the disjointed parts of territories populated by Serbs, Milosevic pursued a systematic policy of ethnic cleansing through genocide and forced relocations.[1]

Colonel Ryland was sickened by the reports of war rape that were part of the policy of ethnic cleansing. So-called "rape camps" were set up to impregnate Bosnian and Croatian women in an effort to produce a new generation of Serbians. Since children inherited their father's ethnicity, this was used as a method of ethnic cleansing. According to one report as many as fifty thousand women, mainly Muslim, were raped during the Bosnian Wars. In addition to the camps, women were gang-raped in the streets and in their homes in front of their families.[2]

Throughout 1995-1998 competitive nationalisms spiraled out of control again. Politicians fanned the fires of all of the old divisions: Serbs versus Croats, Orthodox Christians versus Catholics, Catholics versus Muslims, etc. In September 1998, the United Nations Security Council stepped in to force another ceasefire. Chairman of the Joint Chiefs, General Shalikashvili, played a vital role in planning the air campaign in Kosovo. Colonel Ryland felt fortunate that he picked her to be part of the planning staff. She admired the general for a variety of reasons, not the least of which was his status as the first foreign born Chairman of the Joint Chiefs.

NATO began to prepare for an air campaign in Kosovo in the event that the parties didn't stop fighting. It had been reported that over 230,000 people had been displaced from their homes by Serbian security forces and the Yugoslav Army.[3]

In late 1998 it looked like a UN-controlled solution was imminent, but negotiations ultimately broke down. In March 1999 NATO began a bombing campaign that led to the withdrawal of forces from Kosovo and establishment of a UN mission. A total of 31,600 U.S. personnel participated in the campaign. The operation lasted from March 24 to June 10, 1999.

U.S. casualties were light. Two Army warrant officers were killed in an Apache helicopter accident after the bombing ended.[4] One Air Force F-16 pilot was killed.[5]

Rachel came across the names of the three military casualties as she read through the accident reports a her office in the Pentagon. She was stunned to recognize one of the names. Later that night, she told Bob of her discovery. "I was reading the names of our casualties from the bombing campaign. An F-16 pilot by the name of Captain James Maldonado was the one combat casualty. He was the son of my old boss at Fifth Air

Force, Colonel Maldonado. I told you about him, remember? Or, maybe I didn't."

"I remember you mentioning him, I guess."

"When I worked for him at Yokota, his wife had recently divorced him and he really missed his kids. He had a reputation for being a womanizer, but I think it was unfounded. He actually turned out to be a pretty good boss. This was his only son who was killed."

"What a tragedy," Bob remarked. "How odd that you happened to know the father of the one Air Force casualty in the whole U.S. bombing campaign."

"There was something else I recall from my tour at Yokota. Do you remember those North Korean abductions I told you about? There was one case that especially touched me. It was a Japanese schoolgirl whose brother was a Japanese Self Defense Force officer at Fifth Air Force. The girl just disappeared while walking home from school one day. Her case was never solved."

"I wish there was some way we could assist those Japanese families who have lost loved ones to North Korea. But it won't happen on Clinton's watch," Bob said.

"You're right about that," Rachel said. "Maybe when we get a Republican president you can raise the issue. I hope so. Something needs to be done."

CHAPTER 29
San Francisco

IN CONTRAST TO THE LACK of strategic vision of the Clinton administration, the Republicans promised a new foreign policy with an emphasis on building and sustaining alliances and coalitions. At the height of the presidential campaign, Senator Bob Ryland flew to San Francisco to touch base with his constituents and to campaign for Texas Governor George W. Bush.

They had sold their Vallejo house when they moved to Washington. Their nephew, Will, was living in their vacant San Mateo townhouse while attending San Francisco State College.

"Hey, Uncle Bob," Will said. He met the senator in the foyer with a grown-up handshake followed by a mutual bear hug.

"How's it going, Will?" Bob asked as he gave the living room a quick glance to check on his nephew's housekeeping. He was pleased to see their carefully selected furnishings were still intact and apparently unscathed by whatever activities his nephew inflicted upon them.

"I've been doing summer school trying to get ahead of the power curve for next year. Is Aunt Rachel coming out too?"

"No, unfortunately she's too tied up at the Pentagon. But I'll be here for three weeks while Congress is in summer recess."

"Going to be campaigning for Bush I hear."

"You bet. Your dad tells me that you've been active in the College Republicans. How would you like to help me during your spare time?"

"I'll be glad to stuff envelopes or something."

"I'm going over to your folks' house for dinner tonight. Want to come?"

"I would but I've got a date," Will said sheepishly, looking down at his feet.

"I see. Anyone special?"

"Yeah, I think she's pretty special."

"See if you can recruit her to help at campaign headquarters."

That night Bob was enjoying after-dinner coffee with Harm when the subject of Will's girlfriend came up.

"Have you met this girl yet?" Bob asked. "Yes, we have," Harm answered, eyeing his brother closely. "Her name is Beth Richardson."

"Catherine's daughter?" Bob asked as he almost spilled his coffee.

"The very same."

"How is Catherine, do you know?"

"She got paroled in '93 and went back to finish law school. She's working at the San Francisco courthouse as a public defender now, specializing in family law," Harm said.

"That sounds like Catherine," Bob said, his expression unreadable. "I've always wished I could have prevented what happened. You know she called me the night of the shooting. I volunteered to come over, but she said she'd be okay. I knew she was scared."

"I remember. You testified at her trial. That guy was a real piece of work. She was doomed from the first time she went out with that psycho."

Lost in his memories, Bob didn't respond.

"Did you ever tell Rachel about Catherine?"

"Yes, I did actually. I was so upset about her being sent to prison I told Rachel the whole story. We were just friends, you know. It wasn't like we were having an affair."

Connie came in carrying two scrumptious looking dessert plates. "How about some coconut cream pie?"

"My favorite," Bob said.

She laid the plates down. "Enjoy."

The conversation turned to politics for the rest of the evening. As a political reporter for the *San Francisco Chronicle*, Harm was even more involved in the Bush campaign than his brother.

On the drive back to the townhouse Bob couldn't stop thinking about Catherine. He was glad to hear she was doing well and wondered what excuse he could come up with to visit the downtown courthouse.

When Beth returned home from her date with Will Ryland, her mother was propped up in bed reading a law brief. Beth had grown up to be an attractive, intelligent young woman. Catherine was grateful that her daughter didn't seem to have been scarred by the events of her childhood. She credited this to intensive counseling and the solid upbringing given to her by her grandparents. Beth was majoring in social work at San Francisco State where Will was majoring in pre-law

"Hi, honey," Catherine called as she heard her daughter come in. "Have a good time?"

"Oh, yes!" Beth replied standing in her mother's bedroom doorway. "We went to that new Brad Pitt movie. He's such a hunk.."

"Almost as good-looking as Will?" Catherine teased.

"Will does have the same boyish charm," Beth replied with a small smile. "Did I tell you Will's uncle, the senator, is home for a few weeks?" Beth was oblivious to her mother's prior relationship with the senator.

"Hmm," Catherine said struggling to keep her voice even. She felt her heart kick up at the thought of seeing him again. She tried to cover her emotions with a glib comment. "I'd rather spend August here than in D.C. too."

"I'm going to bed, Mom. See you in the morning."

After saying good night, Catherine laid aside her brief and got out of bed to get a glass of water from filtered tap in the kitchen. She knew Will Ryland was Bob's nephew, but she never told Beth that she'd known Bob in law school. She didn't anticipate their paths ever crossing again. She thought about the last time she'd seen him. He'd come to her sentencing hearing, but she only caught a quick glimpse before they led her away. His face was full of pain. He'd written to her once while she was in prison trying to keep her spirits up. She asked him not to write again. Bob had been off limits from the start. She knew it would be less painful for both of them if they left their friendship in the past. Now her daughter was unwittingly providing a pathway into her former life.

CHAPTER 30
Reunion

"**B**OB RYLAND! OR *SENATOR* RYLAND, I should say," the district attorney for Alameda County said as he approached his former colleague at the San Francisco County courthouse.

"Hello, Graham, good to see you!"

"What brings you to San Francisco?"

"Summer recess in Washington. Time to get back to my constituents and take the pulse. Going to give a few speeches for Governor Bush while I'm in town."

"You always were a great campaigner. I've got a case coming up in a few minutes, but why don't you call me in Oakland and we'll get together some time while you're here?"

"I'll sure do that," Bob replied. He remembered Graham Greenberg as a barracuda of a prosecutor. They were always on opposing sides but had mutual respect for each other. For some reason Bob began to regret his presence in the courthouse. The anticipation of seeing Catherine seemed to have caused an erratic beating in his chest. Just as he was leaving he saw her coming up the courthouse steps.

"Hello, Bob," she said trying to sound calm. She was not surprised to see him. as Beth had already mentioned he was in town. She noted that his silver hair made him look very distinguished. He looked at her with the same lake blue eyes that had always calmed her in the past. Not this time. She stood still and forced herself to relax.

"Catherine," he said as he stopped awkwardly amidst the flow of people. She seemed smaller, shrunken somehow. But her smile was the same one he remembered from years earlier. She was wearing a light gray suit with a crisp white blouse. Her brown hair now had threads of grey. She wore it in a smooth French twist secured by a tortoise shell comb.

"I feel like we're meeting for the first time again," she said, juggling her briefcase and shoulder bag. "You ran into me on the steps of the law library and I dropped my books. Remember?"

"Déjà vu," Bob replied. "Are you on your way to court?"

"I have some time. I was just going to my office. Do you want to come? We have coffee."

He followed her down the hallway, no longer caring that he didn't have a legitimate reason to be at the courthouse except to see her.

"I'll put my briefcase down and get the coffee. Cream, two sugars, right?"

"How could you possibly remember that after all these years?" he marveled.

She smiled to herself as she went to the secretary's office and filled two Styrofoam cups. She didn't spill a drop despite her nerveless fingers.

"Here we are," she said as she set his coffee on the edge of the desk, where he could collect it without risking the touch of her hand.

"It's been a long time, Catherine. You've come through fine," he said, hating himself for such an inane remark.

"It's been fifteen years, Bob."

"Prison must have been almost unbearable."

"I thought I'd die at first. The humiliation, the shame. I felt I was losing my humanity. You learn to live with the noise, the smells, the lack of privacy. They try to make you as miserable as possible. It's supposed to be miserable—it's prison. But no one can steal your freedom in here." She laid her hand on her chest.

"I guess you have to experience it to really understand," Bob offered.

"I don't think about it anymore, but I don't forget about it. Every client I defend will experience the same pain if I don't do my job well," Catherine said. "It keeps me motivated."

"Harm told me you're specializing in family law."

"I'm not a crusader for battered women, if that's what you're thinking," she said, although she'd had her share of battered women clients.

"No, I didn't think that," he said, although that wasn't entirely true.

"So, tell me what's it like being a senator?"

"Busier than a one-armed paper hanger," he joked. "Seriously, I feel that my entire life experience has prepared me for this role. As you know I thought my life was going to be spent in the military, then later I thought I'd continue flying as an airline pilot. Then after the crash I couldn't continue flying. I found my calling in the legal profession. By serving in Congress I hope to use my background and experience to make better laws."

"It can't be an easy course to follow."

"You're right. Politicians can be pretty brutal to each other. It's not for cowards."

"How is Rachel?"

"She's a brigadier general now," he replied, proud of her recent promotion. "She's working for the chairman of the Joint Staff in strategic planning."

"All that separation was worth it, then?"

"Yes. But I must be keeping you from work, and I have to get over to Bush campaign headquarters. I'm scheduled to make a speech to the troops." Bob set his empty cup on the edge of her desk where he had claimed it minutes before. Catherine rose from her chair and saw him to the door of the outer office. He took her hand in parting and said, "I'm so glad to have seen you again, Catherine. Please be well."

"You too," she sighed. He turned, and she watched him walk briskly away.

CHAPTER 31
War on Terror

SENATOR RYLAND AND HIS FELLOW Republicans got their wish in 2000 when George W. Bush was elected to the presidency. Less than nine months later the terror attacks of 9/11 changed the country's perception of itself forever. The war on terror had begun.

At 7:59 a.m. on September 11, 2001, American Airlines Flight 11 took off from Boston. Senator Ryland was in his office pouring over a new bill. His wife, the general, was conferring with her special assistant at the Pentagon.

Less than an hour later Flight 11 crashed into the North Tower of the World Trade Center, killing ninety-two on board and hundreds inside the building. Senator Ryland heard about the crash from one of his aides. They were watching CNN in horror as a second airliner crashed into the South Tower.

While everyone's focus was on New York City, a third airliner had been hijacked. American Airlines Flight 77 had taken off from Dulles International Airport at 8:20 a.m., and terrorists ordered the pilots to head for the Pentagon.[1]

Key leaders from the House and Senate were evacuated to a secure location away from Washington. Senator Ryland called his wife.

"Rachel, are you watching the news?"

"Yes, it's unbelievable."

"It's chaotic here. Key people have evacuated to a secure unknown location."

"Are you staying?"

"That's my plan for now."

A huge concussion cut short their conversation. Rachel hit the floor. The room momentarily filled with bright light and then went to pitch black. A small fire started to burn somewhere in the E-ring. Then a tidal wave of fire rolled down the corridor, coming right for her.

Coughing, Rachel turned away from the smoke and fire and groped her way back into her office on her hands and knees. The sprinklers came on, which kept the smoke and heat down. Oddly, there was no sound. She heard no screaming. The acrid odor of aviation fuel filled her nostrils. For a moment she thought, *I'm going to die.* Then, she said defiantly, "*No way* am I going out like this." She took a couple of shallow breaths and continued to crawl around in the smoky darkness with her face to the floor like a puppy sniffing for crumbs.

A shadow ran by in the dark corridor. She thought of calling out, but the figure was quickly swallowed by the smoke. Where were her coworkers? Why was she alone? The wet carpet beneath her knees became slippery tile. She realized she was in the corridor. In spite of her confusion she was finally able to find her way out of the building.

Emergency vehicles filled the parking lot. Her face and forearms were badly burned. A medic saw her and took her to an ambulance.[2]

Months later Rachel was still wearing flesh-colored compression sleeves on her arms while the burns healed. Plastic surgery was performed on the left side of her face. Her scarring was minimal thanks to the expertise of the doctors at Walter Reed. In the end, she chose to retire at last.

CHAPTER 32

Afghanistan

THE PRESIDENT VOWED TO SEEK out and destroy Al Qaeda and other terrorist organizations in Afghanistan, where the Taliban government was harboring Osama bin Laden, the mastermind of the 9/11 attacks. In keeping with his foreign policy agenda, President Bush immediately formed an international coalition to fight terrorism.

As a member of the Senate Armed Services Committee, Bob Ryland consistently voted to provide the best possible supplies and equipment needed to ensure victory.

Despite the initial defeat of the Taliban regime by U.S. special operations forces, the CIA, and Afghan fighters, the U.S. failed to replace the Taliban with a strong central government. As a result, fighting broke out among the warlords just as it had after the Soviets left a decade earlier.[1]

"Snatched from the jaws of victory," Rachel remarked to Bob, commenting on the shift of the administration's focus from Afghanistan to Iraq in 2003.

"The Afghan people are worse off now than they were under the Taliban," Bob replied. "We're going to be there for years and years. It's another Vietnam."

"Those who fail to learn from history are doomed to repeat it," his wife said, paraphrasing George Santayana.

"It looks like I'll be going on a fact-finding trip to Afghanistan soon," Bob said without enthusiasm.

"You're not getting discouraged, are you?" Rachel asked.

"Why can't this country ever learn how to fight a war to win?" he cried in dismay. His handsome face was contorted into an unattractive mask of anger.

"Sometimes we do," she countered with practiced calm. "When politicians give our generals clear objectives, we're successful. Just look at Panama. Or look at how we dealt with the attempted coup of Corazon Aquino in the Philippines."

"One of the reasons I decided to run for the Senate in the first place was because I was so incensed by the mishandling of the Vietnam War. I thought if enough of us veterans could get elected to Congress we could change things. What we need is a president who has the military experience of Colin Powell and the statesmanship of Margaret Thatcher."

"And the courage of Golda Meir," his wife added with emphasis.

In the spring Bob Ryland was part of a Senate delegation on a fact-finding trip to Afghanistan. The main purpose of the trip was to investigate the management of Defense funds. The delegation met with the top military leaders, as well as Afghanistan's prime minister and other government officials. Senator Ryland's focus was on current military strategy, which he thought was not conducive to victory.

As the small military transport plane turned sharply over Kabul, it began to dive almost straight down. This maneuver was to protect the plane from antiaircraft fire. It was less than thrilling to the civilians on board with the exception of Senator Ryland, whose years of combat flying in Vietnam made the flight seem almost routine.

A new government had been established in Afghanistan. Elections were held in the fall of 2003. Violence levels were down and the military was making progress but as the Bush administration shifted their focus to the threat from Saddam Hussein in Iraq valuable momentum was lost. Bob Ryland had a queasy feeling in the pit of his stomach. After the formal meetings were over, Senator Ryland wanted to get a firsthand look at the way the war was being conducted. He asked to tag along on a routine mission to resupply forces located at Bagram AB northwest of Kabul.

The MH-53M transport helicopter took off in the early dawn. It was the last day of the delegation's mission. The sun glanced off the rotor blades in a starburst pattern. The thirteen members of the aircrew were in an upbeat mood. Senator Ryland enjoyed watching their camaraderie. Less than an hour into the flight a compressor problem caused one of the two engines to stall. The one remaining engine couldn't support the heavy weight of the aircraft in the thin mountain air.

Major Brian Woodley shouted to his copilot, "Jettison the auxiliary tanks."

The copilot tried repeatedly to do so without success.

"We've got to lighten the load or we're going in!" Woodley cried. "Prepare for emergency landing!"

The crew members and Senator Ryland prepared themselves for what looked like an inevitable crash. Then the second engine stalled. The helicopter fell two hundred feet to an uneven riverbed, rolled over, and burst into flames. Miraculously, eight survived.[2] Ryland wasn't one of them.

Rachel Ryland was in her home office working on a speech she was to deliver to a group of College Republicans when she received an unexpected visit. Her old friend from Yokota, Chaplain Delaney, now stationed at Andrews AFB, stood at the door of their Watergate apartment. At first she was pleased, then it hit her: He was on an official visit. It was a death notification.

"Father Delaney," she said tonelessly while opening the door. Her face had lost all its color. "It's Bob, isn't it?"

"Yes, Rachel. I'm so, so sorry. We don't have many details yet," the chaplain explained. "All we know is your husband has been killed in a helicopter crash near Kabul."

"Was it due to hostile fire?"

"Some kind of mechanical failure."

"I want to know how this happened! I want every detail," the general raged, pacing the room as if she could change the outcome by wearing a hole in the carpet. Their Watergate apartment was only minutes from the Pentagon. She was sure she could get more information if she were still on active duty. Father Delaney could only tell her the few details he had been given. She calmed her impotent rage long enough to thank him for coming. It wasn't until she picked up the phone to call Harm and Connie that she began to break down.

With the time difference it was still morning in California. "Rachel, this is an unusual hour for you to call," Connie said, innocent of the impending blow.

"Connie, there's been a helicopter crash near Kabul," she began, then her throat closed and she couldn't wrest the next words out of her larynx.

"Oh, Rachel! It's not Bob!" Her voice broke up in sobs.

"Yes. It was some sort of freak mechanical failure. Five of the crew were killed. Bob was along as an observer. Apparently some of the crew miraculously survived, but Bob didn't. I don't have any more details right now. I just wanted you to know right away. I'll call you back later tonight when Harm's home. By then I should have more information."

"I can't believe this happened. It's such a waste!" Connie moaned, listening for a reply which never came. Rachel had hung up the phone, unable to endure another moment of conversation.

The senator's body and the bodies of the helicopter aircrew were brought back to Dover AFB, Delaware, where they were cleaned, processed, and prepared for burial at Arlington National Cemetery. The flag-draped coffin of Senator Robert Ryland was placed in the sanctuary of the National Shrine of Our Lady of the Immaculate Conception. Father Delaney conducted the funeral Mass. Rachel sat in the front pew flanked by Harm and Connie and their two sons. Afterward, none of them remembered any part of the service.

An honor guard preceded a horse-drawn caisson carrying the coffin to the cemetery. A folded American flag was presented to Rachel. A bugler played taps, and then it was over. Rachel thought her life was over as well.

Two weeks later, still numb with grief, the general had no strength to make any decisions. She had a vague idea about moving back to the townhouse in San Mateo. There was no reason to keep the Watergate apartment. Then the governor of California called. He explained that by law he could appoint her to fill Bob's vacant Senate seat. She asked for some time to think it over and called Harm.

"I don't think I can do this. I can't even begin to think of it. All I can think about is how we wasted all those years when we could have been together but endured separation for the sake of the *mission*. I didn't even know that it was within the governor's power to appoint me in the first place."

"In the early years of Congress it was known as the widow's succession and they only served until the next election," Harm explained. "But in the twentieth century thirty-eight widows won their husband's seat in subsequent elections. You've probably heard of Margaret Chase Smith. She succeeded her husband and went on to serve in Congress for thirty-two years. By the way, in 1964 she was also the first woman to run for the Republican presidential nomination."

"I might have known you'd be able to come up with the historical facts, Harm. How long do I have to decide? The governor didn't tell me."

"In the House they have to have a special election. It's only in the Senate that the governor can make an appointment. Based on that I'd say you don't have to decide right away."

"I wonder if those other widows were in the same of a state of shock I am."

"The governor is probably just asking you now so that you will have plenty of time to think it over."

"My first reaction is not just no, but hell no! I was looking forward to being retired and just being a wife for a change!" Rachel's voice caught as she said this.

"I know. Why don't you fly back to San Francisco while you consider the governor's offer? Connie and I would like to be with you. We all loved Bob. It's a shock to us too. We can comfort each another."

"I might do that. Everywhere I look in this apartment I see Bob. We hardly ever lived in the townhouse in San Mateo. It's not filled with so many memories. I'll call you in a day or two and tell you what my plans are."

"Fine. Talk to you soon. We love you," Harm said.

"You too."

Rachel spent a month in California. For the first week all she could do was wander around the house weeping. Talking to Harm and Connie was helpful but mostly she just raged at her circumstances. Why did God allow this to happen? Why after all the mutual sacrifices they'd made were they now separated once again only this time it was permanent. She was always very independent but she didn't like losing her life long partner. Her independent spirit had seen her through in the past, but she had always been supported by Bob's love for her.

When she couldn't sleep he did housework at all hours of the night. She obsessed over the smallest detail. No corner of the ceiling or floor was left untouched. Cobwebs tended to form in the unoccupied house. She could clean the cobwebs out of her house but she couldn't seem to get them out of her mind.

When she had worn herself out she would collapse in bed and finally sleep. If it weren't for Connie supplying her with frequent casseroles and homemade bread she wouldn't eat at all. She had no desire for food. She neglected her grooming. She had no energy to take care of herself. When she caught a glimpse of herself in the bathroom mirror one day after the first two weeks in California, the reflection looking back at her was just a shadow. Her cheeks were sunken. Dark circles like smudges of charcoal appeared beneath her hazel eyes which had turned light grey. The burn scars from her 9/11 battle with fire at the Pentagon were becoming more visible. She could not see anything positive about herself, her circumstances or her future.

"God, I just want to die!" she raged. She couldn't think about anything except death. Why did Bob have to take that helicopter ride? It wasn't part of the itinerary for the congressional party. "You just couldn't resist being out there as part of the operational mission, could you?" She looked at pictures in their shared study of the early days in her husband's Air Force career. There were several shots of the Academy. She stared at him in his parade dress uniform on graduation day. She hadn't met him then, of course. He was so beautiful. He towered over his fellow cadets, almost too tall for a fitgher cockpit. The F-105 fighter bomber was just big enough for him to fit his six foot two frame into.

On the opposite wall of the study were pictures of Rachel's career. Her favorite was taken by Bob just before her third parachute jump. She was standing by the side of the U4-B with it's open fuselage. She was in full rigging with her gloved hands resting on the belly reserve chute. Looking out beneath her helmet her eyes were clearly focused, her smile was subdued but confident. The third jump was her perfect jump. Not even her nemesis, Chief Holder could find anything to critique. She was intensely proud of her accomplishments at the Academy. Completing the jump program was the hardest thing she ever tried to do—until now.

As she scanned the glory wall her eyes rested on a picture of the cadet chapel with its 17 spires. During the ATO training program just as in the cadet training daily Mass was offered in the chapel before breakfast. It was the one place that felt safe. No one could put you in a brace there and slam you up against a wall and ask you to recite "knowledge," or perform push-ups when you failed to recall some fact.

Rachel turned around and faced the opposite wall again. It struck her for the first time that Bob had hung the same shot of the cadet chapel. She sank to her knees holding both hands over her bowed head in shame. "Oh, God. I'm sorry for my anger. I'm done with being angry at you, at Bob, at my circumstances. I'm sorry for wanting to die. I'm a coward. I've lost my faith. I'm undone. Help me!"

During that time with Harm and Connie's help she sorted out the pros and cons of the governor's proposition. She prayed about it. Father Delaney's words spoken so long ago returned to her. "All we can do is trust, by doing our duty one day at a time, and leave the big picture to God."

She had become involved in Bob's work on a day-to-day basis during the two years of her retirement. She knew the issues on which he was working. Knowing that God uses our weakness to teach us patience, Rachel thought maybe God had a plan in the midst of all this agony. In the end she didn't think it would be honorable to refuse to serve. She accepted the appointment.

CHAPTER 33

The Senator

IN JANUARY 2004 RACHEL RYLAND was sworn in as senator. At first she was filled with apprehension. It wasn't that she didn't feel up to the job intellectually. She was just numb emotionally. It was hard to care about being a politician. Once she became involved in the issues, however, her emotions began to thaw.

Most people assume that in order to become a general one must be politically astute. Rachel was an exception. She never had the inclination to manipulate others. As a senator's wife she had no illusions about the way the political system worked. She'd seen it firsthand. She never wanted to be a politician. Even though most of her professional military peers thought she was all task, Rachel was equally good at relationships. Nevertheless, she felt as vulnerable as a second lieutenant right out of OTS. She needed a mentor.

One morning she was sitting on a sofa outside the Senate chamber while the leaders were arguing over some procedural issues. She was soon joined by Republican Senator Barbara Belmont, a twenty-year veteran of the Senate whom Rachel had admired from a distance.

"This is the damnedest place, isn't it?" the veteran senator murmured. She had a striking, fine-boned face. Her silver-white hair was piled on top of her head in a loose bun. She carried herself with the grace of a high fashion model. She was never seen without a strand of perfectly matched Oriental pearls, which she wore as a choker around her long thin neck.

"Not any worse than the Pentagon, I guess," Rachel replied.

"Maybe not. But the players are probably a lot sneakier," Belmont observed. "There are three kinds of players here. There are the team players, game players, and star players."

"Sounds familiar."

"No doubt. The team players are the workhorses. The game players are the trick horses, and the star players are the horse's hinnies."

Rachel let out a quick laugh. "Are the work horses the ones who get reelected?"

"It's always worked for me," Belmont replied.

Senator Belmont proceeded to take Rachel under her wing. She was the widow of a Navy pilot who'd been shot down toward the end of the Vietnam War. It gave them a common bond.

They both sat on the Armed Services Committee, the one place where Rachel felt comfortable as she was well acquainted with the Defense budgeting system.

Senator Hillary Clinton also sat on the Armed Services Committee. She didn't recognize the retired general from their Wellesley days, which was fine with Rachel.

Clinton had not aged well. She had pouches under her eyes and wore her gray-blond hair in an unbecoming low ponytail. Even in a designer pants suit, she looked like a mobile pup tent. Rachel could still fit into her Air Force uniform. She found some polyester rayon serge material and had several navy blue pants, jackets, and skirts made up in classic lines. Instead of a regulation light blue blouse she wore white open collared blouse or a silk shell. She felt more self-confident in the guise of an Air Force uniform. Her high cheekbones were not marred by Hillary-like luggage under her eyes. In spite of her struggles throughout her career in the military, her facial expression was as fresh as the day she graduated from Officer Training School.

Rachel shared with Senator Belmont her common past with Hillary.

"Watch yourself around Hillary," Belmont said. "She's a barracuda. People assume she's a supporter of women, but she'll sell you down the river faster than you can say Whitewater."

"That's no surprise to me. She's always been addicted to power. I felt sorry for Bill when he was president. She so obviously wears the pants in that family. Do you think she'll make her bid for the White House in 2008?" Rachel asked.

"Of course."

"Let's pray the Republicans can field a candidate who is strong enough to beat her."

"Or that someone more unscrupulous than Hillary will win the Democratic primary so that the Republican candidate will provide an even clearer contrast," the elder senator remarked. "But then, maybe there isn't anyone out there who is more unscrupulous than Hillary."

"There is that," Rachel replied with a wry grin.

Rachel thought she was prepared for the glacier-like slowness of the legislative system, but she was still surprised by the inertia. When she first tried to get a bill through committee she realized she'd never fully appreciated the frustration her husband had often expressed.

On day over lunch in the Senate dining room Senator Belmont set her straight on that. "Honey, it isn't supposed to work well. If it did we'd make a hell of a lot more bad laws. It's a process of natural selection. Only the strongest bills make it through committee, the behind-the-scenes bargaining, the votes on the floor, and the joint conference, and finally make it to the president's desk."

The first piece of legislation Ryland initiated she co-sponsored with Senator Sam Brownback of Kansas. It was the North Korean Human Rights bill. For over twenty years Rachel had been looking for a way to help Japanese abductees. The bill took over two years to pass. After being amended several times it ultimately became law. In May 2006, six North Koreans were granted refugee status by the United States. Four of them were women who had been victims of forced marriages. Eventually, the sister of Ryland's Japanese colleague at Yokota was returned to Japan.

After 30 years of following orders it felt good to initiate something which could truly make a difference in people's lives. Rachel had always thought of herself as pro-active and was a creative problem solver. Working on over 120 issue papers on the problems of the first women at the Academy had hard-wired her ability to think outside the box. As she became acclimated to the role of senator she felt well prepared to make a unique contribution to the nation.

CHAPTER 34
Primaries

AFTER SERVING FOUR YEARS IN the Senate, Rachel was drafted by the Republican Party to run for president in 2008. There was a wave of distrust of career politicians spreading throughout the country. Even a war hero like Senator John McCain was not considered the best possible candidate as he had spent more time in politics than he had in the Navy. Ryland represented a new kind of politician. Unlike McCain, she wasn't associated with the constant shifting sands of power. She wasn't tarnished by the bickering and backstabbing that normally went with a career in politics. She was endorsed by many of the senior military officers with whom she had served. Other military veterans in congress recognized her potential as a national leader.

Harm had retired from the newspaper and served as her campaign manager. Her two nephews, Will and Sandy, were heavily involved as well.

Toward the end of the campaign Senator Ryland gave a speech in New Hampshire that was a rallying cry to all Americans. Speaking about the dire state of the economy, she contrasted her policy of cutting taxes with her opponent's policy of "spreading the wealth around."

"I know you're worried," she said. "We are at a moment of crisis in this country. We are faced with many important questions. Will we continue to lead the world's economies or will we be overtaken? Will we continue to have the strongest military on the planet, or will Defense spending continually be cut in favor of domestic spending?

"The choice you make in November has never been more critical. Americans have always been fighters. I ask you to join me in the fight to keep America strong. Fight to get rid of the corrupt, self-serving, and egotistical political class that has taken over in Washington. Fight for the ideals that have made America great. Fight for your children's future. Stand up and defend our country from its enemies both foreign and domestic! Stand up! Stand up and fight with me for the values of our founding fathers!"

The crowd immediately stood up and erupted in thunderous applause.

Throughout the campaign Senator Ryland had been called a "dark horse" and her election was considered a long shot. She was running against an African-American senator from Illinois. He was well ahead according to the polls despite her standout performance in the debates. When she was elected, no one was more surprised that she. Harm had dubbed her an American Golda Meir. Rachel's fighting spirit often reminded him of the Israeli prime minister's mantra, "Only those who dare, who have the courage to dream, can really accomplish something."

Epilogue

Inauguration Day, 2009

MR. PRESIDENT, MR. CHIEF JUSTICE, fellow Americans, I stand before you today with humility and pride—humility in the wake of those who have gone before me and pride in being an American.

Since its founding, our country has been engulfed in turmoil and uncertainty. As your president it is my preeminent duty to nurture the spirit of the country. This is a role which comes naturally to women. Throughout history women have been seen as "keepers of the flame." In Ancient Greece the goddess Hestia was the keeper of the sacred fire of hearth and home. She was the most influential and widely revered of the Greek goddesses. The living flame of Hestia was tended constantly and never allowed to die out.

What has become of the American spirit? Is it still burning? Or have the values of our forefathers vanished in the wilderness? Has the flame of the American spirit somehow been melded to the myriad, intricate inner workings of a computer? What has happened to the old truths of the heart? Does anyone even ask anymore: What is truth?

Truth is not relative; it is absolute. Truth is eternal and immutable like the figure of a woman on a Grecian urn— forever pure, forever beautiful, and forever loved. As Noble Prize winner William Faulkner said, "Truth covers all things that touch the heart: *love and honor, pity and pride, courage and sacrifice.*"

Our tragedy today is not that we face the loss of material things but that we face the loss of our spirit. What are the enemies of the spirit? Criticism of our country from within and without quenches the spirit. I'm not talking about honest appraisal. We always need that. I'm talking about demanding, disparaging, degrading, brick batting, scorching criticism. Riots against perceived or real racism, sexism and perceived or real abuse by those in power have divided us in the past no less so than in the present. We must rise above our differences. Americans have always valued rugged individualism. Our constitution is based on the rights of the individual. But when we reduce our vision to our own self-seeking concerns we cannot join the greater cause. Americans love a winner. We all love the big league ball player, the fastest runner. We love to belong to the winning team. None of us has the strength to wade through this vale of tears alone. We need the support of one another. Let this be a new beginning for our nation.

When I was a child some people built fallout shelters in their backyards. The only question of that era was: "When will I be blown up?" That is still the question today and it is still the wrong question.

Fear is one of two basic emotions. The other is love. It is natural to be afraid. Fear is triggered by the drive for self-preservation. Only two things can come from fear: courage or hatred.

What is courage? Courage means confronting your worst fear and doing your duty anyway. Courage is born of love—love of God, love of country, love of family. Courage leads to faith, and faith is the antidote to fear.

I refuse to surrender to fear in all its forms: fear of frailty, fear of oppression, fear of annihilation. To overcome fear we must first face it. We must acknowledge it as a part of our humanity. Having done so, we must reject the negative consequences of fear. We must refuse to succumb to anger, hatred, and despair.

Americans have always chosen courage over hatred. When necessary we have not and shall not fail to deploy our physical power, but we will do so with wisdom, consistency, and selectivity. We are heirs to the greatest forces on earth, not just physical power but the power of *love and honor, pity and pride, courage and sacrifice.* Without a belief in these things, any achievement of ours is doomed to be as empty and forgotten as the carcass of an outmoded computer tossed into a landfill.

Standing on the battlefield of Gettysburg 150 years ago, President Abraham Lincoln spoke of heroic sacrifice. He spoke of the need to dedicate ourselves to the cause for which the heroes of that war gave their last full measure of devotion. It is for that same cause the heroes of our modern wars have fought: the cause of freedom. There is no freedom without courage. There is no victory without suffering.

Among the numberless white rectangles of stone across the river from where we are standing is the "Tomb of the Unknowns" guarded twenty-four hours a day, 365 days a year. On the front of the tomb are three images: in the center stands *Victory*, always portrayed as a female figure. On the right stands a male figure symbolizing *Valor*. On the left stands *Peace*. The famous aviator, Amelia Earhart, wrote, "Courage is the price that life exacts for peace."

I will make it a top priority to reinstate the Pledge of Allegiance in our public schools. Future generations of Americans will be lost without it. We are one nation, under God, indivisible, with liberty and justice for all. And let us never forget it!

On the eve of an important battle toward the end of World War II, a great-uncle of mine told his troops, "I don't want to get any messages from the front saying we are holding our position. We're not interested in holding onto anything except the enemy." To do that takes not only physical courage but moral courage.

Let us not grieve for those who have died. Rather, let us thank God that such men and women have lived. We have all loved and lost members of our immediate and extended families. There is not a single American alive today who has not faced the fear of loss. The latest reduction in force puts the family breadwinner out of a job when they turn forty and are the most vulnerable. The greed of banks seeking to inflate the housing market for short term profits end up leaving families without adequate housing as their loans are foreclosed upon. Or labor unions go on strike for a righteous cause such as the Air Traffic Controllers strike in 1981. In spite of the fact that these people held the safety of the nation's air travelers literally in the palm of their hands, an uninformed and ill-advised president made the precipitous decision to fire every last one of them leaving the airways in the hands of others less competent to carry out their tasks.

Let us now witness a rebirth of the American spirit. We must all be keepers of the flame. The real battlefield isn't on the front lines in Iraq or Afghanistan. And it isn't even on the assembly lines of factories or in the loan offices of banks seeking to make a profit. The real battle is in the hearts and minds of each one of us.

The real battle is a moral battle. It is in our own families, our neighborhoods, our churches and synagogues. It is in our town councils and our state legislatures. The real battle is for adequate employment, and good healthcare.. The real battle is against poverty in all its forms, against ruthless, cut-throat business practices, against unfair labor unions that exploit the fears of their members. The real battle is for adequate educational opportunities for all our children.

We are all called to be heroic warriors in this battle. Let us encourage one another. Let us remember who we are. We are Americans. We live by the truths of the heart: *love and honor, pity and pride, courage and sacrifice.* As your president I pledge to hold high the torch of the American spirit. I will never let us forget the values of our founders. We live in a free country with a government *of the people, by the people, and for the people* and, by God's grace, it shall not perish from the earth.

Notes

Chapter 1
[1] Elinor Burkett, *Golda*, New York: Harper-Collins, 2008, 29.

Chapter 3
[1] J. McCullough, "The First Female Astronauts," *Ms. Magazine*, January 1973, 54-55.

Chapter 4
[1] J. Lever and P. Schwartz, *Women at Yale*, Indianapolis: Boras-Merrill, 1971, 120.

Chapter 5
[1] Details were based on description of a simulated aircraft emergency in Stephen G. Keshner, *Cockpit Confessions of an Airline Pilot*, St. Augustine: Booksonnet.com, 4.

Chapter 10
[1] "United Flight 173," retrieved from "http:www. en.wikipedia.org/wiki/United_ Airlines_ flight, 173," 1-2.
[2] Ibid, 2.
[3] Ibid.

Chapter 12
[1] "Tornado," *Wichita Falls Times Record News*, April 11, 1979, 1.
[2] Ibid.
[3] Ibid.

Chapter 16
[1] John F. Farrell, "Team Spirit," *Air and Space Journal,* fall 2009, 1-24.

Chapter 21
[1] Based on a real account in "Abduction of Japanese Citizens by North Korea," Tokyo: Report of Ministry of Foreign Affairs of Japan, 2013.

Chapter 24
[1] Eliza Ogden Hereford, Lake Shoji to Elton Shaw Ogden, San Francisco, September 24, 1904, in the author's possession.
[2] "Fuji Five Lakes," retrieved from "http://www.Japan-Guide.com," 2015, 1.

Chapter 25
[1] "Earthquake," *Time Magazine.* October 30, 1989, 16.
[2] "A Brief History of the 60th Air Mobility Wing and Travis AFB," *Air Force Document 131217-079.pdf,* Travis AFB: Office of History, 2014, 10.

Chapter 27
[1] "60th Air Mobility Wing," 12.
[2] "National War College," retrieved from http://nwc.edu/, 2.

Chapter 28
[1] "Yugoslav Wars," retrieved from http://www.en.wikipedia.org/w/index.php?title= Yugoslav_Wars&oldid=478226777, 3.
[2] "Sexual and Gender Based Violence in Conflict: A Framework for Prevention and Response," UN Office for the Coordination of Humanitarian Affairs, 2008.
[3] Tim Judah, "Yugoslavia: 1918-2003," retrieved from http://

bbc.co.uk/history/worldwarone/yugo- slavia_01.shtml, 4.
[4] "1999 NATO Bombing of Yugoslavia," retrieved from http://www/en.wikipedia.org/wiki/NATO_ Bombing_of_ Yugoslavia, 8.
[5] In 1995, F-16 pilot Captain Mark P. "Mac" McCarthy was lost over the Adriatic Sea during the war in Bosnia. In 1999, F-16 pilot Scott O'Grady was shot down over Kosovo and later rescued. Literary license was used to combine the two incidents.

Chapter 31

[1] "9/11 Terror Attacks Timeline," retrieved from "http:// www.history.com/topics/9-11-timeline," 1.
[2] Based on eyewitness account of Colonel Michael Beans, retrieved from http://9-11research.wtc7.net/pentagon/ evidence/witnesses/b art.htm;#witnesses, 2-3.

Chapter 32

[1] "History of Afghanistan," retrieved from http:// en.wikipedia.org/wiki/History_of_ Afghanistan, 18.
[2] "United States Helicopter Crew Killed in Afghanistan," retrieved from http://www.arlingtoncemetery.net-/ chopper-crew-november-2003.html, 3.

Acknowledgments

NO AUTHOR WRITES ALONE. I am no exception. I am indebted to all those who helped me to believe in the story as I went along. In particular, I want to thank my sisters, Suford Lewis and Linda Hamilton, for reading the early drafts and providing feedback. I also am indebted to members of the Christian Writers Guild who taught me how to write from a Christian perspective.

There is no way to measure the impact that moral support brings to the creation of a story. Along the way I was encouraged by many friends. Burt Strubhar inspired me to never give up. Fellow author Cort Sutton reviewed portions of the book and provided excellent feedback.

I also recognize those who reviewed the manuscript and wrote endorsements. My good friends Colonel Robin Grantham, USAF (retired) and Colonel Frank Urbanic, USAF (retired) provided the professional military viewpoint in their reviews, which are printed on the back cover.

The most important step in bringing this story to print was the design of the book cover. For that I am indebted to my niece, Alice Lewis, who is a graphic designer and an experienced professional in book layout and design.